"My brother confided in you about my niece?" Emily asked, surprised.

Drew shrugged. "I was he— ... good listen... responsibili... ...ard."

Emily bit he... ...with kids and coa... ...ually have any kic... ...own.

He drummed his fingers on the table. "My mom. She raised my brother and me by herself. Of course, as a kid, I had no appreciation for all she did for us."

So that's where his voice of experience came from. Why was she so quick to shoot him down?

Drew reached across and lifted her chin. "We could double-team your niece. My experience with teenage boy soccer players and yours with persnickety clients and temperamental artists. What better qualifications for handling a sullen teenage girl?"

"Sure. Sounds like a plan."

Although right now it seemed more like a recipe for disaster.

JEAN C. GORDON's

writing is a natural extension of her love of reading. From that day in first grade when she realized *t-h-e* was the word *the,* she's been reading everything she can put her hands on. A professional financial planner and editor for a financial publisher, Jean is as at home writing retirement and investment-planning advice as she is writing romance novels, but finds novels a lot more fun.

She and her college-sweetheart husband tried the city life in Los Angeles, but quickly returned home to their native Upstate New York. They share a 170-year-old farmhouse just south of Albany, NY, with their daughter and son-in-law, two grandchildren and a menagerie of pets. Their son lives nearby. While Jean creates stories, her family grows organic fruits and vegetables and tends the livestock du jour.

Although her day job, writing and family don't leave her a lot of spare time, Jean likes to give back when she can. She and her husband team-taught a seventh-and-eighth-grade Sunday school class for several years. Now she shares her love of books with others by volunteering at her church's Book Nook.

You can keep in touch with her at www.Facebook.com/JeanCGordon.Author, www.JeanCGordon.com or write her at PO Box 113, Selkirk, NY 12158.

Small-Town Sweethearts
Jean C. Gordon

Love Inspired

Recycling programs
for this product may
not exist in your area.

™ LOVE INSPIRED BOOKS

ISBN-13: 978-0-373-87720-1

SMALL-TOWN SWEETHEARTS

www.LoveInspiredBooks.com

Printed in U.S.A.

Dear Reader,

Welcome to Love Inspired!

2012 is a very special year for us. It marks the fifteenth anniversary of Love Inspired. Hard to believe that fifteen years ago, we first began publishing our warm and wonderful inspirational romances.

Back in 1997, we offered readers three books a month. Since then we've expanded quite a bit! In addition to the heartwarming contemporary romances of Love Inspired, we have the exciting romantic suspenses of Love Inspired Suspense, and the adventurous historical romances of Love Inspired Historical. Whatever your reading preference, we've got fourteen books a month for you to choose from now!

Throughout the year we'll be celebrating in several different ways. Look for books by bestselling authors who've been writing for us since the beginning, stories by brand-new authors you won't want to miss, special miniseries in all three lines, reissues of top authors and much, much more.

This is our way of thanking you for reading Love Inspired books. We know our uplifting stories of hope, faith and love touch your hearts as much as they touch ours.

Join us in celebrating fifteen amazing years of inspirational romance!

Blessings,

Melissa Endlich and Tina James
Senior Editors of Love Inspired Books

In memory of my dear sister-in-law Carol Gordon,
who inspired me to write this story.
You are sorely missed by all of us.

Also to my husband, Mark,
who puts up with all of the oddities and
inconveniences of being married to a writer.

And to my critique group, BFS.
You know who you are.

* * *

For where two or three come together in my name,
there am I with them.
—*Matthew* 18:20

Chapter One

The thrumming in her head started at the Essex County line and crescendoed into a pounding by the time she'd reached State Route 74. She wiped one hand, then the other on her jeans and gripped the steering wheel of her rented SUV. She was in control. She was Emily Hazard, assistant art director at an award-winning New York City advertising agency. Not Emily Hazard, the klutz-queen jinx-deluxe of Schroon Lake Central High School.

She drove through Hazardtown, the four corners community in New York's Adirondack Mountains that her ancestors had settled two centuries ago. Little remained to show the bustling logging town it had once been. A new name on the diner told her it had changed ownership again. The gas station convenience store proclaimed Souvenirs Here in a big red, white and blue roadside sign. Kitty-corner, the Community Church sat as it had for the past one hundred and fifty years with its double entry doors that had originally separated the women parishioners from the men. As a teen, Emily had made a point of entering through the men's door. The newish brick volunteer fire department building occupied the fourth corner. Ironically, the old clapboard hall had burned down when she was in college.

Paradox Lake came into view on the left. A patch of blue nestled in the greens and browns of the hardwoods and mountains surrounding it. Her heart beat double-time. As she came around the curve to Hazard Cove Road, a mama duck and her ducklings waddled onto the highway. She hit the brake pedal and sensed the pickup truck behind her before she heard the screech of its brakes. The truck touched the back bumper of the SUV and nudged her forward just short of the little family.

She pulled over onto the shoulder of the road, closed her eyes and let her chin drop to her chest. *Don't let it be anyone I know. Please don't let it be anyone I know,* she pleaded. Raising her head, she glanced in the side view mirror. The pickup driver had pulled over behind her. A tall, dark-haired man in a flannel shirt and jeans stepped out and approached her, stopping to check the front of his truck and the back of the SUV. From the rearview mirror, Emily couldn't see any real damage to the truck. She squinted at the mirror. Maybe a tiny dent in the bumper. Hopefully, the damage to the rental car was equally minor.

She pressed the door-lock button. Five years of living in the city had taught her to be wary of strangers, even in little Paradox. Maybe more so in Paradox, where she still knew at least ninety-five percent of the population. And this wasn't anyone she knew.

She grabbed the car rental agreement from the glove compartment and rolled her window down a notch when the man reached the door. He looked pleasant enough. Faint laugh lines bracketed his mouth. But the set of his jaw and the wariness in his light blue eyes neutralized any overt friendliness his half smile might seem to offer. Her pulse raced. This wasn't her fault. Hitting the ducks was *not* an option. She breathed deeply. At least she wasn't obsessing about being in Paradox anymore.

"Are you okay?" the man asked.

"Yes, I'm fine. And you?" She took in the set of his broad shoulders. He looked fine. Better than fine. She tapped the steering wheel with her pointer finger.

"I'm good." He shrugged those shoulders. "It's just a fender bender."

"Yeah. How much of my fender is bent? It's a rental."

"Hop out and take a look."

She glanced back. Another man was getting out of the pickup. "Um, maybe we should just exchange insurance information and call the sheriff's department for a report. I'll need it for the rental company." She cringed inside. Whatever officer came, chances were good that it would be someone she'd gone to school with. So much for her quietly slipping into town and keeping to herself.

The second man approached the SUV, his face shaded by the shadows of the trees. Emily tensed, now wishing that someone she knew had rear-ended her.

"Jinx!"

Relief flooded her as she recognized her brother Neal. She'd even forgive him for using her hated nickname—this time.

"I wasn't expecting you for a couple of hours."

Emily rolled down the window. "I got an early start and I was driving against the commuter traffic into the city, so I made good time." She crooked her head toward the other man.

"Oh, yeah. This is Drew Stacey, the guy who's renting the campgrounds. We were dropping my truck off at the repair shop. My sister…"

She glared him a warning.

"My sister Emily."

"Emily." Drew nodded. "Do you want to check out the damage now?" The corner of his mouth quirked up.

The guys moved away from the door so she could step out. Emily felt Drew's eyes on her as she walked to the back of the SUV and resisted the urge to brush herself off. For all she knew, the wrapper of the granola bar she'd eaten on the trip up was stuck to her behind.

"Oh, no," she said when she saw the dent in the bumper. If it had been her own car, it would have been minor. With a rental car, it was definitely damage. She exhaled forcibly. "I'd better call the sheriff."

"No need," Drew said from beside her.

"Look at that dent."

He looked up over the car. She followed his gaze. A county sheriff's cruiser was headed down the highway toward them.

"Ken Norton makes his rounds about this time every day," Neal explained.

Of course he did. Deputy Norton always had. No reason for her to think anything might have changed here in Paradox. At least it wasn't one of her former classmates ready to mock her propensity for disaster. The father of one of her classmates *was* one step removed.

The cruiser passed them, made a U-turn and pulled ahead of the SUV. The deputy got out of the car, a broad smile creased his weathered face. "Jinx Hazard," he boomed. "I heard you were back in town."

A male chuckle followed. Emily turned toward her brother and Drew. Both appeared innocently straight-faced.

"I may have said something at church," Neal admitted.

Her stomach dropped. He might as well have taken out an ad in the local paper. No, wait, announcing her visit in church probably reached more people.

"What have we got here?" Deputy Norton flipped open a pad and pulled a pen from his shirt pocket.

"I…" Emily and Drew both started at once.

"You first." Norton gestured to Emily. "License and registration."

Emily handed him the rental papers she had in her hand and dug her license out of her purse.

Deputy Norton looked them over and handed them back. "What happened?"

"I stopped to let a duck and her ducklings cross the road and he rear-ended me." She folded her arms.

The deputy glanced over at the lake side of the road. The mama duck and her babies were long gone. He scribbled on his pad and pointed his pen at Drew when he'd finished. "I need to see your license and registration, too."

Drew pulled his wallet from his back pocket and handed over the documents.

"New York City," the deputy read out loud. "You up here on vacation?"

Emily caught the note of outsider suspicion in Deputy Norton's voice. Her spirits lifted. She *did* have the hometown advantage. Good for something.

"No, sir," Drew answered. "I work for the coalition of churches that's rented the Lakeside Campground for our summer program. I'm up here early to get the old lodge in shape for us to use."

"I heard Neal was having some renovations done. You've got your work cut out for you," the deputy said. He turned to Neal. "When's the last time the lodge was open?"

"Fifteen, maybe twenty years ago. Dad said it didn't pay to keep it open anymore with all the newer hotels around. People prefer their RVs or the house cabins."

"It was quite the place when we were kids. Your dad and my high school class had our senior prom there, you know."

The words "senior prom" made Emily cringe.

"Are you all right?" Drew asked.

"I'm fine," she answered.

"You went kind of white there for a minute like you were in pain. You're sure you're not hurt?"

She relaxed. The concern in his eyes seemed genuine. "A little shaken up," she said. But more from being back in Paradox than from the accident. "I really am all right. Thanks."

He favored her with a smile that released the rest of her pent-up tension.

"Ahem." Deputy Norton cleared his throat. "These look in order." He handed Drew back his license and registration. "So, what happened here?"

"I came around the curve. Didn't see her until it was too late," Drew said. "I couldn't brake fast enough. You know, there's usually no traffic this time of day."

The deputy checked out the front of the pickup and the back of the SUV and wrote some more. "How about you, Neal? What's your take?"

"What Drew said. We came around the curve. He wasn't doing more than forty-five, fifty tops, and there she was."

"You weren't with your sister. You didn't see any ducks?" Deputy Norton asked.

Emily's temper flared. Did he think she was lying?

"No, I didn't," Neal answered. "All I saw was the SUV in front of us."

"How about you?" the deputy asked Drew.

"No, but I was kind of busy trying to stop the truck."

Deputy Norton jotted another note in his pad and flipped it shut. "Looks like a no-faulter to me."

"No one's fault!" Emily uncrossed her arms and placed her hands on her hips. "There's a Slow Curve sign before the curve and the road's posted to watch for deer. People know you can't careen down this road. What if it had been a deer instead of my car?" She felt Drew's gaze on her and she couldn't meet it for the remorse flooding through her. She'd repaid his concern for her by dumping all the fault on him. But she couldn't have run the ducks down.

"Then, we'd have a mess. Lynn will have the report typed up by tomorrow, if you want to bother with insurance claims."

Like she had a choice. "It's a rental."

"I'll make sure Lynn gets right on that report. You can

pick it up at the station. And I'll let Matthew know you're in town."

His son, Matt. Great! The class president, football team quarterback who had invited her to the senior prom on a dare from a teammate. Unknown to her until they got there. She shuddered at the memory.

"He and Becca just had a baby. My first grandson," Deputy Norton said. "I know they'll want to see you."

Becca Morgan. Former head cheerleader and debate team captain. She and Matt would want to see Emily about as much as Emily wanted to put her life in New York on hold to be here in Paradox. They should enjoy a laugh about her grand return.

"Good seeing you, Jinx. Meeting you, Drew." Deputy Norton tipped his hat and walked back to his cruiser.

Neal's and Drew's goodbyes to the deputy faded into a brief hushed conversation. Neal approached her and draped his arm over her shoulder. "You're sure you're okay?"

She nodded.

"Drew thought you were acting funny. But I told him no, that's just you."

Yeah, that's me, funny-acting Jinx Hazard. "Thanks, bro."

"What?"

"Nothing. It was a long drive. I'm tired."

Neal opened the passenger door of her rented SUV. "Hop in. I'll drive us to the house."

She opened her mouth to argue that she was perfectly capable of driving, then relented. Why not? It had been a long drive. "Sure." She slipped into the passenger seat.

He waved his intention to Drew and took over the driver's seat. Drew pulled his truck out ahead of them and was around the next curve before Neal had even started the SUV.

Emily clutched her purse. That's why Drew had been so concerned about her. He knew he'd been going too fast. She rested her head on the back of the seat and closed her eyes to let go of her irritation with him. So much for the quiet, uneventful arrival she'd planned.

Drew drove up a side road to Lakeside and stopped in front of a log home just inside the campground. He parked in front and climbed out, locking the door behind him, though it was probably unnecessary. But old habits die hard. As Drew often had since he'd arrived at Paradox Lake, he imagined what it would have been like to grow up here in the Adirondacks instead of the cramped apartment in Brooklyn he and his brother had shared with their mom.

Now he had a new element to add to that picture. Jinx Hazard. No, he'd better make that *Emily* Hazard. His survival instinct told him they'd get along a lot better if he didn't call her Jinx. And a very interesting element it was. Tall and willowy thin, Emily was a study in contrasts with wide-set gray eyes that would have given her face an open, welcoming look if not for the shadows flickering there. Unlike most of the women he knew in New York, she hadn't messed with the color of her honey-brown hair. And the haphazard way she'd pinned it up didn't jibe with her perfectly fitting designer jeans and soft hoodie sweater. He didn't miss that it was a sweater, not a sweatshirt.

The mischievous part of him that his mother had worked so hard to control had wanted to pull the clip holding her hair and see how far it would tumble down her back. At least halfway was his guess. It wasn't the echoes of his mother's reprimands that stopped him. It was Emily's attitude. The expression on her face when first her brother, then the sheriff deputy had called her Jinx told him that, for her, growing up at Lakeside Campground might not have been the idyllic experience he pictured. One thing for certain, she did not share his enthusiasm for being here.

* * *

When Emily opened her eyes, the first thing she saw was Drew's pickup parked in front of the house. Her heart flip-flopped. "He didn't have to stop over," she said as much to herself as to her brother. "I told him I was fine."

"Don't you remember? I offered to let Drew stay at the house in the room over the garage until he has the apartment in the lodge in shape to move in there."

Emily did a quick mental review of the many phone conversations she and Neal had had over the past few weeks. He might have thrown a lot of things her way in his efforts to get her to agree to look after Autumn while he was on his tour of duty with his reserve unit. But that one she would have remembered.

She shifted in the seat. "It's not a good idea. You know the people here. They'll talk."

"Come on. It's not like it'll be the two of you alone in the house."

Right! Her seventeen-year-old niece as chaperone.

"You don't even know him, Em. He's a good guy. You'll like him."

Whether she liked him or not didn't matter. Or, maybe it did. She couldn't deny the hint of attraction she'd felt when she'd thought he was concerned about her being hurt. But it would look better if she didn't like him. "Neal, this is hard enough for me already. I'm not sure how I'm going to manage my job working from 250 miles away. I can't handle the Paradox rumor mill as well."

"It's not that bad," he cajoled. "Most everyone knows he's been staying at the house and that you're coming to stay for Autumn."

"That doesn't make things better."

"We can't sit out here all afternoon."

He opened the door and got out. "You're too sensitive.

Don't you think it's about time you got past high school? Everyone in Paradox is not out to get you."

"I *have* gotten past high school." Her family had never seen how bad it had been for her.

He closed the SUV door with a force that said "end of conversation" and walked to the back of the vehicle to unload her things.

Emily climbed out and joined him. She knew she should give him a break. He had a lot on his mind. His deployment. Not seeing Autumn for who knew how long. Emily staying with Autumn. Emily didn't flatter herself that she was Neal's first choice to take care of his daughter. A far third was more like it, after her parents and Autumn's maternal grandparents. But Emily had been Autumn's choice, and Neal had always had a hard time saying no to his daughter.

Of course, Emily was Autumn's choice because she was the only one who could stay with the teen in Paradox Lake. Autumn was adamant about finishing her senior year at Schroon Lake Central High with her friends, even though she'd been accepted in the early enrollment program for January at Trinity College in Chicago where her other grandfather taught. Emily couldn't understand how Autumn could give up an opportunity like that. Was she the only one who felt stifled by small town life? One more way she didn't fit in.

She joined Neal who stood with the cargo door open staring inside the SUV.

"You know the house *is* furnished," he said.

She slugged his shoulder playfully. "That's my computer and workstation."

He grabbed the molded plastic desktop and pulled. "How did you get this in here?"

"I have friends, male friends."

He straightened. "Em. I didn't think about that. Is being here interfering with anything, um, special?"

She wished. "No, why? Are you filling in for Mom?"

"You, too? She's none too subtle about wanting more grandchildren. Frankly, for me Autumn is more than enough."

"Hey, I heard that." Autumn sprinted toward Emily arms open. Emily hugged her close, surprised as she always was at how tiny she was. Autumn took after her mother, not the Hazards.

"Hi, squirt."

The teen released her and stepped back. "Aunt Jinx. I'm so glad you came. You don't know what it's been like here with nothing but men."

The big grin Autumn had for her dad and Drew, who had followed her out of the house, belied her complaint. She'd always had her dad wrapped around her little finger. Emily could only imagine she'd done the same with Drew.

"Need some help unloading?" Drew asked.

"Drew." Autumn's voice bubbled with enthusiasm. "This is my Aunt J—Emily," she corrected herself.

"We've met."

"Well, duh, you must have since Dad left with Drew and came back with you." Autumn grabbed Emily's hand. "Come on. Let's go in. We've got to talk."

"My stuff."

Autumn waved toward Drew and Neal. "The guys can get it."

"It'll go faster if we help." Emily reached for one of the boxes.

"No, you go ahead in," her brother said.

Emily took the box anyway and followed her niece to the house and into her past. The kitchen was exactly as it had been when she'd left for college eight years ago. Even the dish towels looped through the ringed door pulls on the cabinets under the sink seemed to be the same. She walked down the hall to her old room. Her stomach churned as she opened the door. She breathed deeply. *I'm only visiting. This is tempo-*

rary, she chanted silently. She placed the box at the end of the bed where it would be out of the way until she unpacked it.

"So, what do you think?" Autumn asked.

"About what?"

"Drew, of course. Isn't he hot?"

"He's a little old for you." Emily deflected the question.

Autumn rolled her eyes. "I know that. Besides, I have Jack. Although a girl can look."

Yeah, Jack, the car mechanic Autumn had been dating far too long in Emily's opinion, an opinion she'd shared with Neal. She suspected Jack was a large part of Autumn's choosing to stay here rather than go to Trinity College this past January.

"I meant for you," Autumn said emphasizing her words as if Emily might not get her meaning. "And you didn't answer me."

"He seems nice enough."

"Nice enough?"

"Okay, he's good-looking if you like that rugged, outdoor look."

Autumn favored her with that look of disgust all teen girls seemed to have in common. "Not city enough for you? You know he's from Manhattan."

Yeah, Emily had caught that when Deputy Norton was questioning him.

"He used to work on Wall Street or something. So does that make a difference?" Autumn asked. "Do not judge, or you too will be judged. Matthew 7:1." She grinned. "I've been practicing for the Bible in Real Life competition at youth group. You have to come up with a verse to match a situation."

"No." Emily smiled with her. "It doesn't make a difference." It didn't matter, not really. Manhattan or not, Drew wasn't her type. If she had a type. She'd been uniformly unlucky with all types of men. That was one aspect of her "jinx" she hadn't been able to shake in college or New York.

"Hey." Neal poked his head in the room. "Where do you want us to set up your desk and stuff?"

"I thought I'd work in the spare bedroom over the garage." Drew appeared behind Neal.

"Oh, that's right. It's being used." She glanced around her room. "I guess we could put one of the twin beds in the attic and I could work in here." She'd really hoped she'd be able to separate her work and private space.

"Can work wait a couple days?" Neal asked.

"I guess." It was Friday. She didn't have any pressing deadlines and she could check her email on her iPhone to stay connected.

"Good. Drew can move into my room when I leave."

Lovely. The room next to hers.

"He can help you set up your stuff in the room over the garage. There's plenty of space with the sofa bed folded up. And we won't have to move any furniture."

"I don't want to put anyone out. I can move to one of the motels. It's off-season. There are lots of rooms available," Drew offered.

Emily shifted her weight from one foot to the other. Drew's thoughtfulness was nice. She *would* feel more comfortable with a little distance between them.

"No, man," Neal said. "We talked about this. The campground is too secluded this time of the year. I'd rather Autumn and Emily not be out here by themselves."

She bit her tongue. She lived in New York, by herself. But Neal was just being protective of his daughter.

"Yeah, we want you to stay," Autumn said. "Don't we, Aunt Jinx?"

The smile that tugged at the corner of Drew's mouth stabbed Emily like a blade.

She drew on the counseling she'd gotten at college. *He's*

laughing at the situation Autumn's put you in. He's not laughing at you, she repeated until she'd gotten things back in perspective. "Sure, it's always good to have a man around the house."

"Good. That's settled," Neal said. "I'll bring the rest of your stuff in from the car and let Drew go back to work. Thanks for the lift from the garage."

"Anytime."

"And thanks for helping Neal haul my things in," Emily said.

Drew nodded. "See you later."

Emily watched him stride down the hall with her brother. It wouldn't be bad. Drew would be working at the lodge and she'd be working in her office upstairs. They'd probably hardly even see each other. And she'd disabuse Autumn of any matchmaking ideas she might have in her head—no matter how attractive he was.

Chapter Two

"That's the last of it," Neal said, placing a large suitcase on the bed next to the smaller one she'd just finished unpacking.

Emily smiled. Neal wasn't bad as brothers went, not bad at all. The kind of man who could make some woman very happy. Too bad Autumn's mother had done such a job on his head that he hadn't pursued any serious relationships since. She closed the bureau drawer and flipped open the top of the suitcase.

"You didn't have to haul all my stuff in yourself. I could have—we could have helped." She tossed Autumn in, too. It wouldn't have hurt her to lend a hand.

"It's all right. Where is she?" He looked around the room as if he'd just noticed his daughter wasn't there.

"The phone rang."

His features tightened into a look she recognized all too well from their dad. "She'd better not be making plans for tonight." His expression softened. "You remember. The guys from the VFW in Ticonderoga are giving the unit a send-off party."

She remembered and would prefer to skip it, not that she'd share that thought with Neal. "Sure thing." Emily bent over the suitcase so he wouldn't see the tears gathering in her eyes.

"Hey, what's wrong?"

"It's kind of scary."

"True. Being responsible for a teenage girl is very scary."

She punched him playfully in the shoulder. "No, you big lug. Your going to Afghanistan is scary." She dropped the pair of pants she'd lifted from the suitcase and hugged him.

"Come on." He stepped back out of her grip and lounged against the door frame. "You're as bad as Mom."

"No one is as bad as Mom. How did Easter go anyway?" She'd avoided asking Neal about his and Autumn's trip to Florida to spend the holiday with their folks and grandmother. That way, she felt less guilty about not joining them.

"Not bad. The weather was warm. Mom got to show us off at Easter service."

"Was she very disappointed that I didn't come?"

"Of course, but she got over it."

"I was swamped at work."

"Nobody said you weren't. Besides, I always was the good child," he teased.

"Right," she said, remembering some high school escapades she was sure Neal would rather she not mention. Still, there was some truth in his tease. Helping their parents at the campground, sticking around Paradox Lake for them was just easier for Neal. Besides, he got help with Autumn in return.

"And how is Grandma?"

"As good as can be expected. You really should try to get down to see her."

Emily's mind flooded with all of the good times she'd spent at her grandmother's house in Hazardtown before she'd moved to Florida. "I know," she choked out. "In the Fall." Provided she could get time off work after getting the agency to reluctantly let her telecommute for the summer.

Neal pushed away from the door frame. "I need to run up to the lodge and finish some electrical updates."

"Nothing like putting it off to the last minute." She got in her own shot.

"You know, paid work, unpaid work." He gestured with his right hand, then his left as if weighing the two. "I had to finish up my outstanding electrical contracting jobs first. You might not know it by looking at her, but Autumn likes to eat."

"Go on." She shooed him off.

"I'll be back in plenty of time for the party. Grab whatever you want from the refrigerator if you're hungry. And if you need anything else, just ask Autumn, if you can lure her out of her room."

"I should be okay. I got something to eat on the way up. I'll just unpack and check in at work."

"You haven't even been away a day."

"My email, that's all. I did a big client presentation yesterday."

"No getting wrapped up in something I can't drag you away from this evening." His voice held a hint of warning.

"I promise. I won't miss your send-off party." Even though she could come up with about one hundred and six other places she'd rather be tonight.

"Better not. And I invited Drew."

Great. Now he could see her out in local society at her worst. It didn't matter, anyway. Why was she even concerned about making a good impression on Drew?

"I hope the accident didn't put you off him. He really is a good guy." Neal's eyes sparkled.

So, her brother was matchmaking, too. "Don't go there." He feigned innocence.

"Your daughter has already started the campaign, and with even less subtlety. I can handle my own love life, thank you." He snorted.

"You should talk. When was the last time you had a date?"

"I'm too busy raising Autumn."

"That excuse may have worked when she was small, but she's seventeen and going away to college in a couple months."

"Um, she's going to North Country Community College for her first two years."

"What? She's staying here?" She stared at him.

He shrugged. "It's what she wants, and it'll save me a lot of money. Some of her friends go there."

Yeah, one friend in particular that Emily knew about— Jack. He was taking auto mechanics. "You really—"

Neal cut her off. "We've been over this before. I'm not telling her where to go to college."

"You could encourage her. The State University at Albany or Plattsburgh aren't that far."

"Not everyone is you. Some of us like small town life." His voice was tight. "I'll be back in a few hours. The party is at seven." He turned and left.

Tears pricked her eyes. Why was she always like this when she came home? It wasn't like she hated Paradox. She just felt like she didn't fit in. The last thing she wanted to do today was argue with Neal. He was leaving tomorrow. She bowed her head and blinked the tears away.

"Lord," she started self-consciously even though she was alone. It had been a while since prayer had been a daily part of her life. But desperate times called for desperate measures. "Watch over Neal and his unit and all of the other men and women in our combat forces." She paused. "And give me the fortitude and grace to manage living in Paradox Lake for the next four months."

The cell phone ring broke Emily's concentration. She put down her sketch pad and pulled the iPod earbuds from her ears. Neal's number flashed as she picked up the phone. "Hi."

"Hey. Things are taking a little longer than I expected. I should be home in about twenty minutes."

Emily checked the clock. She had no idea it was so late. "Good thing you called. My client wants some changes to the proposal I presented yesterday. I was working on some ideas and lost track of time."

"Why am I not surprised? Can you check on Autumn and make sure she's getting ready? She takes forever."

"Sure." Emily had been so engrossed in her project she hadn't given Autumn a thought all afternoon. She swallowed hard.

"All right. I'll be home as soon as I can."

Emily put the phone down and made one more adjustment to the concept she'd been sketching before she went looking for her niece. As far as she knew, Autumn was still in her room. When she reached the top of the stairs, she heard the murmur of voices. Either Autumn was still on the phone or watching a DVD on her laptop computer. She smiled. Autumn had been begging Neal for her own computer for the past couple years. Neal had wisely waited until her parents had gone down to Florida to take care of Grandma before getting her one this past Christmas. Their mother was definitely of the school that kids shouldn't be able to hole up in their rooms to watch TV or use the internet.

Emily knocked on Autumn's door.

"Come in."

She opened the door. Autumn and Jack were sitting on the bed watching a movie.

"Hi, Ms. Hazard," Jack said.

She hadn't even heard him come in the house, and she was sure this coziness was not something her brother allowed, despite the nonchalant way they continued to sit there with his arm draped around Autumn's shoulders. Emily let their attitude fuel her temper. It was better than giving in to the sinking feeling in her stomach that taking care of a seventeen-year-old girl might be beyond her ability. She clenched her teeth. If Autumn thought she was going to allow stuff like this to go on, she'd better think again. They might be almost as close in age as Emily and Neal, and they were good friends, but Emily was the adult. The adult who had charge of Autumn while Neal was deployed.

"Jack." She dismissed him with a curt greeting and focused her gaze on her niece. "I just finished talking with your father."

The young couple exchanged a glance, and Jack removed his arm from her shoulder.

"He's going to be here in about fifteen minutes and wants us to be ready to go."

Jack inched away from Autumn and swung his feet off the bed and onto the floor.

"Jack needs to leave—now." Her voice took on a quality of her mother's that she knew only too well. A steely quality that would come in handy when she had a little talk with Autumn as soon as Jack left.

Autumn slid off the other side of the bed. "Jack's coming with us. Daddy said he could."

She studied Autumn's face. The teen's defiant response didn't jibe with Neal's concern earlier that she'd better not be making plans to ditch the party. It bolstered her confidence that Neal was also a little clueless when it came to Autumn. "You can wait downstairs," Emily said to Jack, who was already one step from the doorway.

Emily walked to the computer and pushed the shut-off button.

"Aunt Emily. You're not supposed to shut it off like that with a DVD in it."

She turned back to face her niece. "And I'm sure you're not supposed to be in your bedroom with Jack with the door shut."

Autumn dropped her gaze to the floor. Emily waited for her to apologize.

"You're not going to tell Daddy, are you?"

Emily clenched her hands, and got a grip on her anger. "No, I'm not, as a favor to him, not you. The last thing he needs is to head off to Afghanistan worried about you."

Autumn lifted her head. "Sorry, Aunt Jinx."

"Emily." The correction popped out. She usually let Autumn get away with calling her Jinx.

"Emily." Autumn twisted the name to match the curve of her lips. "We weren't doing anything."

The emphasis she placed on "anything" challenged Emily to contradict her.

"You know. You're younger than Dad. I thought you'd understand that things aren't like they were when he was in high school."

Emily's mind flashed back to the two teens nestled together watching the movie. Her heart started pounding. This was only her first day here. "Go ahead and get ready. Your father will be here any minute now."

"I *am* ready."

Emily appraised Autumn's outfit. Jeans and a long-sleeved striped T-shirt layered with a spring green short-sleeved T-shirt. "The party is casual?" she asked.

Autumn glared at her.

"I was going a little dressier." She'd had her black silk-blend slacks and a turquoise cashmere sweater in mind.

Her niece shrugged. No help from that corner. Emily didn't want to draw attention to herself. Her plan was to slip into the party and stay in the background.

"So is it okay if I go down and check to see if you scared Jack away?"

"Go ahead."

Emily followed Autumn downstairs and left the teens in the living room with her best imitation of her mother's "you'd better behave or else" expression. In her room, she laid the slacks and sweater on the bed. Maybe she should wear jeans. She didn't want to feel out of place. Yeah, jeans would be better. Who did she have to impress? Her mind summoned a picture of Drew expressing his concern after the accident.

"Jinx. I'm back," her brother called down the hall. "I'm going to hit the shower and then you and Autumn can have the bathroom if you need it."

"Okay," she shouted back, smiling to herself. It was just like before she'd left home, everyone jockeying for time in the main bathroom. Dad had never gotten around to connecting the plumbing for the shower in the second bath off the room over the garage until after she'd left home.

Emily checked her reflection in the full-length mirror on the back of the closet door. The jeans and sweater needed something else to dress them up. She dug out a batik scarf and knotted it loosely around her neck. Much better. She pulled out the clip that held up her hair and ran her fingers through the waves that cascaded down her back. Hair and makeup would have to wait for Neal to finish in the shower.

After another glance in the mirror, she headed back to the living room to join Autumn and Jack.

"Nice."

The unexpected male voice brought her to an abrupt stop. Grabbing the frame of the arch between the kitchen and the dining room saved her from falling flat on her face. She breathed a deep breath to slow her pounding heart and jerked her head to the left. Drew stood just inside the door.

"Sorry," he said. "I didn't mean to startle you." His gaze passed over her face and down her hair. "I wondered how long it was."

What was it with men and long hair? She pushed a strand back over her shoulder. "I didn't see you."

"Obviously." He grinned as he sauntered over to the table in the breakfast nook and sat down as if he lived there.

He *did* live here and would be living here—for a while at least. So she'd better get used to it and, if her still-racing pulse was any sign, to not letting her hair down in front of him in any sense of the words.

"Join me?" he asked, pulling out the chair next to him.

"I'm going to check on Autumn and Jack." She kept her tone soft so the teens wouldn't hear her talking about them.

Neal walked up behind her and snapped her with the towel he'd been using to dry his hair. "All done."

"Good." She escaped to the bathroom to put herself together.

Emily gave her lips a final coat of gloss over her lip color and checked out the result. Hair restyled, securely pinned in a loose chignon, makeup flawless. She was armed and ready to face the good folk of Paradox Lake, Drew Stacey included.

"I'm all ready." Emily returned to the kitchen expecting her brother's usual crack about what took her so long. The room was empty.

"Neal went ahead with Autumn and Jack," Drew said as he picked up a pile of clean clothes from the chair next to him, stood, and tucked them under his arm. "The hot water in the bath upstairs isn't working. I'll see if I can fix it tomorrow. Give me five minutes and we can go, too."

Go? With Drew? The two of them? "Ah, sure."

True to his word, he was back in about five minutes. Emily knew because she'd watched the hands of the clock over the sink tick off each minute as she'd paced the kitchen.

"Ready?" His dark hair was still damp, and he'd changed into gray chinos and a loose-knit sky blue sweater that matched his eyes and emphasized his lean, rugged physique.

Her mouth went dry when he stepped closer and the scent of his aftershave assailed her. Understated but tangy. The aroma was so familiar. Certainly nothing her brother would wear. "Nuance," she said.

"Pardon?"

"You're wearing Nuance."

His eyes narrowed. "Yes. How did you know?"

She laughed. "I'm sorry. I did an ad campaign for Simon Stahl. I probably can identify the scent of every one of their products."

"The TV commercials with players from the U.S. National Soccer Team?"

"No. Weren't they awful? I did the print campaign. *GQ, Esquire.* Web design."

He shrugged. "I kind of liked the commercials. They're why I picked up the cologne."

"Oh." The seconds ticked by in silence. "Let me get my coat. It's in the front closet. Then we can go." She ducked into the living room. So much for her being ready to face Drew. What was it about being in Paradox that turned her into an awkward adolescent?

Drew bit the inside of his cheek to keep from smiling until she'd turned the corner. He'd seen her print ads in *Esquire.* They were good, very good. But the temptation to get a rise out of her had been too great. And so easy. He was stymied how she held her own in the rat race of New York advertising. But apparently she did, according to her proud brother.

She returned wearing a long duster-like coat and a guarded expression that had him wanting to take back his tease about her ads. He'd better watch himself. The last thing he needed right now was to get mixed up with another woman. Especially one who appeared to be as changeable as his ex-fiancée had turned out to be.

Although finding out who the real Emily/Jinx Hazard was—cool, collected career-focused art director or warm, endearing klutz—could be interesting. But he'd leave that to someone else. He needed downtime from women to concentrate on *his* career—once he figured out what that was now. Wall Street wonder or that church guy he'd heard some of the locals call him. And that was being generous. In reality, he was a glorified handyman who had to regularly dip into his savings to pay the bills. He doubted that was Emily Hazard's type.

He shoved his fingers through his hair. How had his mind gotten off on this tangent? They'd just met and he hadn't picked up on any signs of interest on Emily's part. Showed how messed up *he* was right now. Drew opened the door and followed Emily out.

"I'll drive," she said.

He half expected her to ask him what took him so long.

"Fine," he agreed. "You know the way better than I do."

Head up, chin forward, she marched to her rented SUV. Her cool expression and his unwanted attraction to her told him it would be a long half hour drive to Ticonderoga.

Chapter Three

The party was well under way when Emily and Drew walked into the VFW hall. A red, white and blue banner proclaiming We Support Our Men and Women in Uniform spanned the room. A few couples danced to a local country western band. Most of the people stood talking in small groups or at the tables arranged around the perimeter of the room. Emily's posture stiffened when a guy across the room smiled at her in recognition. The man approached them with a woman in tow.

"Jinx," the man greeted her.

Drew took in the man's carefully styled blond hair, the cut of his gray suit and the way he held himself. *Financial services.* He judged. *High school, maybe college, sports hero.*

"I heard you made your usual grand entry into Paradox."

"Matt."

Drew almost had to step away to avoid being hit with the tension radiating from Emily.

"Becca," she said to the attractive, petite, dark-haired woman beside Matt. Her facial muscles strained visibly to paste a smile on her face.

"When Dad stopped by the insurance office this afternoon and said—"

Becca placed her hand on his forearm. "Behave yourself."

Surprise flashed in Emily's eyes, as if she wasn't used to anyone sticking up for her. *Interesting.*

"But, Bec, it was classic Jinx. Dad said she stopped to let some ducks cross the road and that church camp guy from New York City plowed into her. Who else would that happen to?"

Both women frowned at him.

"Aw." He squirmed under their combined glare. "Jinx knows I'm only teasing her."

Emily's rigid stance contradicted him. Why was she putting up with this?

"And I would have liked to see the expression on the church guy's face when he came around the curve to see Jinx and her ducks." Matt looked at Drew as if he'd just noticed him. "Matt Norton." He extended his hand. "And my wife, Becca," he added as an afterthought.

Drew nodded at Becca, who looked undecided whether to fade away gracefully or kick her lout of a husband in the shin to get him to shut up. He shook hands with Matt using more pressure than necessary. "Drew Stacey." He paused. "The church guy."

Matt slapped his thigh. "Then, you totally get me. About Jinx and the ducks. Calamity follows her like a dark cloud. Always has, since we were kids."

Drew forced a smile. "No, I don't get you at all."

Matt stood speechless. An unusual state for him, Drew guessed. He caught a glimmer of mirth in Emily's eyes that dispelled any thought he might have about apologizing to Matt for his rude response.

"Hey, isn't that Dan Kennedy?" Becca said louder than necessary. "I want to wish him well before we leave." She faced Emily, her eyes fixed somewhere in the vicinity of her knees. "We're not staying long. The baby. It's the first time we've left him with a sitter other than our mothers."

A genuine smile spread across Emily's face. "Matt's dad told me. Congratulations."

Matt opened his mouth, but Becca squeezed his arm before he said anything. "I'm still on maternity leave from school. Why don't we get together for lunch and catch up?"

"Sure." The word hissed out as if pulled from Emily's lips.

"Great!"

Emily's face took on the hooded, guarded expression he'd seen earlier. *Hmm.* The woman sounded sincere to him. But what did he know? He was the new guy in town.

"Nice to meet you, Drew," Becca said.

"Yeah," Matt agreed. "See you around."

The couple walked off with Becca leading the way.

"Friends of yours?"

She glanced at him out of the side her eye. "Hardly. We went to high school together," she said as if that explained everything.

"Becca seems okay."

"I suppose. We didn't hang together. I don't know why she suggested lunch."

"To be friendly. Make up for her husband." Might as well state the obvious.

"Whatever." She looked around the room as if planning her escape, which seemed to be her M.O. whenever things got uncomfortable.

"Hey." Autumn joined them. "You know Ms. Norton? Isn't she cool?"

"She always was," Emily said, ignoring Drew's raised brow. The party was starting out as she'd feared.

"I wish she was back from maternity leave. The sub we have for Economics is so lame."

"So Becca's a teacher?"

Autumn pursed her lips. "You didn't know that?" she said as if it were universal knowledge. Emily was sure it was if you lived in Paradox.

"I haven't really seen Becca since high school."

Autumn shrugged. "Daddy has a table for us back in the corner. Snacks are over there." She pointed to the left. "And drinks. I was going to get a soda. There's punch, too. Want something?" Her gaze passed from Emily to Drew and she smiled.

"I'll go with you," Drew said. "What can I get you?" he asked Emily.

"A Sprite would be good, if you don't mind."

"Got it."

Emily watched Drew and Autumn cross the room, the teen talking away, gesturing with her hands. Drew nodding. Neal was right. Drew was a nice guy. Putting that obnoxious Matt Norton in his place. Fetching a drink for her. And good-looking, too. Emily didn't miss the looks he was getting from some of the women. It wasn't often Emily attracted that combination in a man. She squeezed her eyes shut to block out the thought. Like he'd shown any signs of being interested her. Besides, she was here to take care of Autumn, not to revive her nonexistent love life, no matter how appealing that might be.

"Excuse me." A shoulder bumped hers. Who had she run into now? And how had she managed to do so while standing still?

"I should have been watching where I was going," the woman said.

Emily turned to see Mrs. Donnelly, her high school English teacher.

"Emily. I heard you were coming back."

"Mrs. Donnelly." She waited for a more refined rendition of Emily and the ducks. The older woman smiled and squeezed her hands. Maybe Mrs. Donnelly hadn't heard about her afternoon escapade. Or maybe she should get over it and not let Matt's comments ruin her evening.

"It's so good to see you. I'm glad so many of my former students are returning to the area."

"I'm only back temporarily, to stay with Autumn while Neal's out of the country."

Mrs. Donnelly continued as if she hadn't spoken. "There's you and Becca Norton. She taught in Syracuse for a while, you know, before she moved back to teach at Schroon Lake."

Emily didn't know. She'd assumed Becca and Matt had gone off to be star quarterback and head cheerleader at one of the state colleges and come right back to Paradox.

"And I'm certain there are others. But my memory escapes me. It's not what it once was. I blame it on retirement. Being with young people keeps you young, I say."

Emily bit the side of her mouth to keep herself from laughing. Mrs. Donnelly's memory got away from her often enough before she'd retired, when Emily was in her class.

Mrs. Donnelly dropped her hands. "I'll let you go. I'm sure there are a lot of people you want to see. Be sure and say hi to my grandson, Josh. He's headed off with your brother. We're so proud of him." The woman's eyes glistened.

"We're proud of them all," Emily said, tapping down the apprehension that blossomed inside of her every time she thought about her brother leaving.

"All right, then," Mrs. Donnelly said. "Let's par-tay."

Emily laughed as the woman trotted off more or less in time to the music. She crossed the remainder of the room without being accosted by anyone else and found Neal deep in conversation with Jack. Reading him the riot act? She could only hope. But probably not from the grin on the younger man's face. Emily weighed whether she should tell Neal about Autumn having Jack in her room this afternoon.

"You found us," Neal said as she approached the table.

Jack concentrated on demolishing the chicken wings on the plate in front of him.

"I did. And it wasn't easy. Mrs. Donnelly caught me mid-room."

"She's already passed this way." Neal looked behind her. "Where's Drew? You haven't ditched him already, have you?"

"No, he and Autumn are getting drinks and snacks. And what do you mean ditched him? That would imply I was with him."

Jack's head shot up. "I could use a drink." He flew off in the direction of the refreshments.

It looked like she had things in hand with Jack. Her brother and Autumn, not so much. She didn't need him setting her up with Drew. She'd have all she could handle refereeing Autumn's love life.

Neal pulled out the chair next to him and she sat down.

"Mrs. Donnelly said her grandson is shipping out with you. He's so young."

"A couple years younger than you. Not everyone in the unit is an old man like me."

Her chest tightened. At thirty-four, he was far from old. Too young to have a daughter as old as Autumn and too young, in her opinion, to be facing the dangers ahead.

He reached over and chucked her chin. "Hey, what's with that long face? This is a party."

Her throat clogged. She caught a tear that threatened to ruin her mascara and her carefully architected image.

"We're back. With food." Autumn's voice rang singsong above the music. She set the plate of appetizers down and scanned the table. "Where's Jack?" Her gaze drilled into Emily's.

"He went to get a drink," Neal said.

"He didn't say anything to me about wanting a drink. I would have gotten it for him." Her eyes narrowed and refocused on Emily. "Didn't you tell him we were getting food?"

"She sure did." Neal came to her rescue. "That's what gave him the idea to go get a drink."

Autumn slid into the chair next to Emily, leaving Drew to take the seat across from her between Neal and Autumn.

"Did you tell Daddy?" Autumn kept her voice low so that only Emily could hear.

"No," Emily mouthed, glancing up to see Drew watching them. She pressed her lips together. No need for him to know their family business.

He slid the soda he'd gotten her across the table.

"Thanks." She took a sip. His gaze held hers for a moment. She broke the hold and shifted in her seat, glad when the band started up a new song and Autumn began tapping the beat on the table.

"Daddy, dance with me. I love this song and I don't see Jack anywhere."

A look of pure pain crossed Neal's face.

The teen released an exaggerated sigh. "I know you hate to dance, but…"

"Come on." Drew stood and motioned toward the dance floor with his head. "I'll go a round with you."

Emily and Neal watched Autumn and Drew join the other dancers in a perfect two-step. Emily wouldn't have pegged him as a good ole boy. He was a man of many talents.

"She's beautiful, isn't she?" Pride showed on Neal's face. "You know she's the same age I was when she was born." He sobered. "I don't want her to make the same mistakes I did."

"You've done a good job raising her." Despite his tendency to spoil her. Of course, her parents had been there most of the time.

"I…" Neal hesitated. "I'd appreciate it if you didn't press Autumn to leave Paradox before she's ready. You know what happened with her mother."

Emily squeezed her brother's hand. "Autumn isn't Vanessa." Not by a long shot from what she remembered of Autumn's wild mother.

"Maybe if I'd given Vanessa more space, hadn't pushed her so hard to stay here with me and Autumn..."

"Like you think I'm pushing Autumn to go away to college." Emily couldn't believe Neal was sounding so maudlin about a woman no one had seen or heard from in more than seventeen years.

"No." He played with the tab on his soda can. "It's that Autumn has made her own plans. She and Juliana are going to rent Jule's aunt's in-law apartment in Ticonderoga and do their first two years of college at North Country Community College. Jule's a good kid and her mother and aunt will keep tabs on them. I'll have less worry about not being here. In fact, Jule's mother offered to let Autumn stay with them for the rest of the school year." He looked up, his eyes clearly conveying his unspoken thought.

"But Jule is Jack's younger sister and that's a little too close for comfort for Daddy," she added.

"You got it." He squeezed her hand back. "I'm so glad you agreed to come."

"I am, too." And to her surprise, she realized she was.

They sat silently for a moment while the band finished its song and moved on to a slow ballad. Emily saw Autumn and Drew start back to the table. Jack intercepted them and Autumn slid into his arms for the dance. Drew turned from the couple, his gaze catching Emily's.

He probably thought she was staring at him. Jack pulled Autumn closer and Emily's embarrassment faded with the fear that she had bigger things to be concerned about. Neal set his jaw.

So Neal had concerns, too. "I'll keep an eye on them," she said.

"Appreciate it. She's still my baby, even if she thinks she's all grown-up."

She teared up again.

"Hey." Drew leaned on the table.

Emily looked up. Her unshed tears softened his chiseled features.

"I'm going to head back to the house and work on my plans for the lodge kitchen. I had an idea out there on the floor. If I don't see you in the morning, take care, man, and watch your back."

Neal stood and they shook hands. "I'm expecting to see the campground a going place when I get back."

What was Neal talking about? He wouldn't be back for a year or more. By then Drew would be long gone. Or was Neal thinking about renting the campground to the coalition of churches on a regular basis? It didn't matter.

Neal sat and Drew smiled at Emily. "I'll see you around."

"Not if I see you first." She bit her lip, but it was too late. The temperature of her cheeks went up a degree for each centimeter his smile dimmed. She'd chalk it up to the Paradox Jinx factor.

Drew raised his hand in half wave. "Don't worry. I'll see you."

Emily caught the smirk on her brother's face. As if she didn't get Drew's meaning.

"Something tells me you're going to have a lot more interesting summer than I am."

She returned her brother's smirk despite the sinking feeling he was right. She had enough going on with Autumn and work this summer. She didn't need Drew to make it "interesting," too.

Chapter Four

Emily stood at the front door watching the reserve unit's van pull out of the driveway.

"God bless," she whispered.

Her fingers tightened on the temporary guardianship papers she held in her hand. Neal had gone over them with her this morning. For better or worse, Autumn was all hers until her eighteenth birthday in August.

Her niece trudged up the cobblestone walkway, head down, blond hair falling forward to hide her face. When had she changed from the little girl she used to read bedtime stories to into this young woman? Emily had let Autumn say goodbye to her father alone. Sure, Neal had gone away before for active duty, and down to New Orleans to help after Hurricane Katrina. But this assignment was longer and different. Emily's parents had still lived in Paradox the other times he'd been gone. And this deployment was more dangerous.

Autumn turned the doorknob, and Emily stepped back out of the way. Cool air hit her face as the door swung into the kitchen.

"Hey, I thought we'd go into town for lunch. What do you say?"

Autumn looked up and pushed her hair out of her face. Tears streaked her cheeks.

Emily reached for her, but she pulled away. "Thanks, but I'm not hungry. I'm going up to my room for a while. Jack's coming over after he's done with work, about two or so."

"Oh, okay," she said to her niece's retreating form. Emily wandered into the kitchen. She didn't feel much like eating, either. As she turned to go down the hall to her room, the door to the garage opened. Her breath caught. No one but family used that door. She released her breath and chided herself. This was Paradox, not New York City. It was probably Jack, although she hadn't heard his car pull in.

Emily turned ready to tell him that she'd appreciate it if he would knock before he walked in.

"Hi."

It wasn't Jack.

Drew crossed the kitchen to her. "Did you want to move your office things into the upstairs room today?"

"No."

"You need some time alone. I get it."

"No. I...no."

He smiled.

She smiled back, realizing how inane she must sound. "I can say more than no."

"It's just that I leave you speechless?"

She laughed uncontrollably, the dam on her pent-up emotions washing away.

He feigned insult. "The idea isn't that funny."

She wiped away the tears and hiccuped. "I've got to sit down."

"See." He pulled out a kitchen chair for her. "I've knocked you off your feet."

"I concede." She collapsed into the chair.

He turned the chair across from her around and sat resting his forearms on the chair back.

She breathed a deep breath. "You don't have to move your things."

He stared at her intently. "I don't think that would work."

"Work?"

"Sharing a room."

"I—"

He grinned. "Seriously, it's no problem for me to move."

She shook her head. "I thought about it. And it's just that… that people might talk."

His brows knit in question.

"The room over the garage is better for you. It has its own entry way and all."

He tilted his head.

"I don't think it's a good idea for you to have the bedroom next to mine."

One side of his mouth quirked up. "I could lock my door."

Maybe she could just slide under the table out of sight. "That didn't come out right."

"No, I shouldn't have teased. Go ahead."

"I got to thinking that Autumn will have friends over and people could get the wrong idea." Her cheeks heated. "And talk. It wouldn't be good for her."

"Or for you," he finished.

Lord knew people were probably talking about her enough as it was. "I'm thinking of you and your job, too."

"I appreciate that."

"What I can do instead is use the dining room. It has good light and, with just the three of us, we can eat here in the kitchen." She stopped. "I assume you've been having your meals here."

"Yeah, I've been kicking in on the groceries."

"You don't have to do that." She was in great shape financially. She'd sublet her apartment, had her salary from the agency, and Neal had arranged for her to be able to draw from his Basic Allowance for Quarters for her and Autumn's living expenses. Drew's job couldn't pay much. Nonprofits rarely did. And if he'd been on Wall Street as Autumn had said, he had to be used to having more.

"Yes, I do." His hands gripped the chair back until they whitened. "I always pay my way."

"Okay, whatever you and Neal agreed." She wasn't going to argue.

"I can go to a motel."

Where did that come from?

"If you're uncomfortable with my staying here." His voice had lost its edge.

She was. Sort of. But not enough to tell him to go. That would leave her alone with Autumn.

"Neal was right. It's better if you're here on the grounds." There, she wasn't exactly saying she wanted him to stay, although part of her did.

His cell phone rang. Saved by the bell.

He pulled the phone from his pocket and glanced at it. "I should take this." He answered the call.

Emily stood and walked over to the sink. She ran water to wash the breakfast dishes and drown out Drew's conversation but heard snippets anyway.

"Things are coming along. Yeah, I made a deposit. Check the account."

Sounded like business. She ran the dishcloth over the plates and stacked them in the drainer, then stepped over to the stove to get the frying pan.

"I don't see why. I told you that I wouldn't be able to get down for Mia's dance recital."

Dance recital?

"Yeah, I miss my boys. I hate to be missing spring soccer."

Drew had kids? He didn't wear a wedding ring. She scrubbed the pan. And Neal and Autumn wouldn't be trying to set her and Drew up if he was married. Unless they didn't know.

"I didn't forget that next Sunday is your birthday."

Was he talking with his wife? The thought made her frown. Maybe she should slip into the living room and let him finish his conversation in privacy.

"Mom!"

He was talking to his mother? She put the pan in the drainer and pulled the sink plug.

"Tell Mia that I'm sorry I missed her recital. She can give me a private show when I come down next Sunday. And I'll talk with Ethan then."

Emily wiped her hands on a dish towel.

"I see. At the market. I know you liked her. You're forgetting that I didn't break our engagement. She did."

Emily hummed to herself as she tucked the dish towel back in the drawer handle. Evidently Drew wasn't married. Maybe he was a widower. A single father like Neal. That could be one reason he and Neal had become such fast friends. The kids must live with his mother.

"Yes, all summer. It *is* a real job. Don't worry. I had no problem depositing the money."

Several second of silence passed. "Love you, too, Mom. I'll see you next Sunday. Bye."

Emily walked back to the table. "I couldn't help overhearing. Will the kids be joining you when school lets out?"

He knit his brow. "What do you mean?"

"Mia, Ethan...your boys."

The furrow deepened and her stomach churned. She didn't normally suffer from foot-in-mouth disease. It had to be something in the Paradox water supply that affected only her.

His expression relaxed. "You thought I had kids?" He favored her with a wry smile. "I have a hard enough time taking care of myself these days."

"Autumn told me you used to work on Wall Street," Emily said, glad for the opportunity to move the conversation into a safer thread—work.

"I was a research analyst." He shrugged. "And I can't say I really miss it."

"So, what do you do for the coalition, besides opening up the summer camp?"

"That's it. This is a temporary gig my brother, the assistant pastor, got me. I think it bothered him seeing me less busy than him. He's always been the more laid-back one."

Compassion filled Emily. Drew must have been pretty desperate to leave New York for the job in Paradox. And apparently he still sent money to his mother.

"Why the face?" he asked.

The Paradox water struck again. She'd worked hard to train herself to mask her emotions, a skill she needed in her work. "Your having to come to Paradox, even if it's only temporary."

"No hardship for me. My brother and I used to come up here for summer camp."

Visiting was different than living here. But she'd stop before she made things even worse. "Summers are the best here."

He looked at his watch. "Want to get going on moving your stuff?"

"Sure. Can you get Neal's toolbox from the garage?"

"On the shelf by the door?"

"That's the one. Meet me in the dining room."

He stood. "And since you asked earlier, Mia and Ethan are my niece and nephew, and the boys are my church soccer league team."

As he crossed the room to the garage door, she admired the way his flannel shirt stretched across his broad back. He was handy, sent money to his mother, was willing to watch his niece's dance routine and coached kids' soccer. Did the man have no faults? Well, he seemed to like it here at Paradox Lake. She could hold that as a strike against him to counter her unwanted interest.

* * *

Drew grabbed the toolbox and headed back into the house. Emily was a puzzle to him. Living in New York, how could she not appreciate getting away to Paradox, even if she didn't want to live here? Sure, the nightlife was very low key to put it mildly, and commercial art jobs were probably scarce to nonexistent. But he had the distinct feeling Emily hadn't liked living here as a kid, either. He couldn't see what there was to dislike from a kid's standpoint. All the outdoors. The security of knowing your neighbors, knowing practically everyone in town. From what he could tell, Autumn seemed to thrive here. She kept busy with school and youth group activities. And from what he remembered there wasn't that much going on for his brother and him in Brooklyn when they were teens, either. If there had been, they probably wouldn't have gotten in so much trouble.

Drew found Emily wedged into a corner of the hallway outside of her room, barricaded by the molded plastic top to her workstation.

"Need a hand?"

"You think?" She pushed back a strand of hair that had come loose from her braid, and he visualized it all tumbled down her back as it had been yesterday when she was getting ready for the farewell party.

He grasped the desktop and slid it most of the way back into her room. "You should have waited for me."

She stepped out and around him without comment. He pushed the piece back into the room and brought it partially out into the hall at the opposite angle, toward the dining room. "Grab the front and I'll lift it. You can guide me to the dining room."

She did as he asked and he lifted the workstation top with a stifled groan. It was heavier than he'd expected. Emily might appear slight, but the woman definitely had some muscle to have wrestled the thing into the hall. They deposited it in the dining room and carried in the other pieces to the workstation and Emily's desktop computer and boxes with her other work things.

"Where do you want the workstation set up?" he asked.

"The left side wall so I'll get the light, but not the glare from the windows. But first, I want to take the leaf out of the table to make it smaller and push it over in the far corner." She motioned past the panel of three double-hung windows to the far right-hand corner of the room.

"You pull one side of the table and I'll pull the other. Then we can lift out the leaf."

"At your command." She *was* commanding. This must be the New York City Emily. He liked her, just as much as going-to-a-party Emily and stop-traffic-for-baby-ducks Emily. The problem was, which was the real Emily? He shook off the thought. It didn't matter. They were nothing more than temporary housemates and he was going to keep it that way. Not that she'd given him any sign that she wanted more than that. She didn't even really want him in the house. She was only honoring her brother's wishes.

The sound of a door opening and closing almost made them drop the leaf.

"Are you expecting someone?" His grip on the leaf tightened.

"Autumn said that Jack was coming over after work. But I don't like him walking in without knocking."

He swallowed. He'd walked in the same door as Jack without knocking.

She lifted her side of the leaf so Drew could get a balanced grip on it. "You can put this over against the wall. I'm going to go talk with Jack."

Emily marched from the room.

Drew did as Emily had instructed and opened the box with the other desk components. A buzz of conversation hummed down the hall punctuated by several staccato words from

Emily that Drew couldn't make out. He smiled to himself. He hoped she wasn't coming down too hard on Jack. From what he'd seen, Jack was a good, responsible kid. He reminded him of a couple of the guys on his soccer team. A pang of regret pricked him. So far, giving up his coaching was the only drawback to taking the job up here. He should check and see if any of the local youth sports teams needed any help.

"Emily went to tell Autumn I'm here. She said I should come help you." Jack scuffed the toe of his Skechers against the box Drew had opened.

"It's Emily now? What happened to Ms. Hazard?"

"She told me to call her Emily before she gave me a lecture about knocking before walking in the house." He glanced over his shoulder as if to make sure she wasn't behind him. "Can you figure her? Autumn always talked like she was real cool."

To Drew, Emily *was* pretty cool. "Take some advice from me," he said. "Never try to figure out women."

Emily and Autumn appeared in the doorway a few minutes later. A frown spread across the teen's face. "I thought we were going into town for lunch."

"This will only take a couple of minutes." Jack helped Drew lift the desktop onto the frame they'd assembled.

Emily bit her lip. Autumn hadn't been hungry a half hour ago when she'd asked her if she wanted to go out to eat. She and her niece had hardly had a minute together since Emily had arrived. She shook off the gloom that was threatening to engulf her. Autumn was a teenager. Sure, she'd rather be with her friends than with her aunt. She and Drew had plenty more set up work to do. After they finished, she could work on the new concepts for her client.

"Go ahead." She waved Jack off. "I can help Drew finish."

"You sure?" Jack ducked under the desk to tighten a bolt. If he wanted to stay, maybe she and Autumn could catch that lunch together. She turned to Autumn who glared at Jack's back.

"I'm sure."

Jack backed out from under the desk and stood. "Want us to bring you guys anything back?"

"Where are you going?" Emily asked.

Autumn transferred her glare from Jack to her.

"The Hazardtown Diner, probably."

"And into Glens Falls to catch a movie, so it would be out of our way to come back here," Autumn said.

Autumn hadn't said anything to her earlier about a movie and, from the blank expression on Jack's face, she hadn't said anything to him, either.

"Uh, right, sure." He and Autumn left.

"And you were concerned about Jack leading Autumn astray."

Had she been that loud? "Well, I'm not comfortable with him letting himself in and heading up to Autumn's room, among other things." She'd better start figuring her niece more into her concerns, though.

Drew nodded. "Did he give you any trouble?"

"No, he seemed agreeable enough coming in here to help you while I let Autumn know he was here."

"But you don't like him."

"It's not that I don't like him. But he's older."

"What, a year?"

Kids who had a year of college seemed so much more mature to Emily than high school seniors did. "Autumn has so much potential. She's smart, talented and beautiful. She could go anywhere, do anything she wants. Jack will probably take over his father's auto repair shop."

Drew's eyes widened.

"That didn't come out right. I'm not elitist. I just think Autumn should see more of the world before she ties herself down here."

"And if she saw more, she wouldn't come back." His lips thinned as if he were sealing in the rest of his thoughts. "You know, Autumn wanted to stay here alone. She argued incessantly with your brother about having to have a babysitter."

Emily felt like she'd been sucker punched. "No, I didn't."

"I probably should keep my mouth shut, but I think you need to know what you're dealing with. I don't know how much time you've spent with Autumn lately, but from what Neal said, they've been at loggerheads since your parents went down to Florida."

Neal hadn't said anything, except that Autumn wasn't happy about him having to go overseas.

"But you were her first choice if she had to have someone stay with her."

"Thanks, I think." What had she gotten herself into?

He positioned the assembled workstation against the wall. "Here good?"

She stared at the piece of furniture without seeing it. She'd call her mother. *And pray hard.*

Drew and the desk came into focus. He looked at her expectantly.

"Yes, that's fine."

"Hey." He pulled one of the dining set chairs over facing him and leaned his hip against the desktop. "I didn't mean to throw you like that. I told Neal he needed to fill you in."

"He had a lot on his mind."

It sounded like Neal had talked with Drew and not her. Or was Drew speculating? "He talked with you?"

"Some." Drew tapped the side of the desk with his fingertips. "He kind of asked me to watch out for you guys. Part of the reason your brother answered the coalition's ad in the Glens Falls paper was because he wanted someone else here at the campground with you and Autumn." Neal had approached the coalition. Not the other way around? *Terrific.* Autumn didn't want her here, and Neal thought she couldn't handle the job, so he'd brought Drew in to babysit her. She'd show them all that she was Emily Hazard, responsible adult, and not Jinx Hazard, calamity waiting to happen.

Chapter Five

Emily climbed the slate steps to the white clapboard church, hoping to slip into a back pew unnoticed. After dropping Autumn off at the Sunday school annex behind the church forty-five minutes earlier, she'd gone back home, rather than hanging around for service. That way she avoided the inevitable invitation to join the adult class. Fellowship was fine—for some people. She preferred to worship privately, one reason she liked the large church she belonged to in the city. She could attend relatively anonymously and make her contributions in cash, rather than time.

Before they'd gone south, someone was always asking Mom and Dad to help with this or that fundraiser, host a prayer group or serve on one committee or another. And they had. They seemed to like it. Not her. Her beliefs were too personal. Besides, keeping up with work and Autumn would keep her plenty busy. And she didn't want to create any ties that could keep her up here a minute longer than necessary.

Emily slipped into an empty back pew and placed the hymnal on her lap. A quick scan of the sanctuary found Autumn sitting with Jule and Jack and their parents, and Drew in a front pew sitting next to a blond she didn't recognize, at least not from the back of her head. His truck had been gone when she'd gotten back from driving Autumn to Sunday school, and she'd figured he'd gone to one of the bigger churches in Glen Falls for service. He certainly must be used to a much larger congregation than the Community Church offered. The woman sitting with him might be the attraction. She tilted her head. Maybe she could recognize her if she got a side view of her face.

Her former English teacher, Mrs. Donnelly, tapped her on the shoulder. "It is hard to see from here. Come on down and sit with me." The older woman took her hand. Emily grabbed her purse and stood. The hymnal fell from her lap with a thud that—to Emily's ears—picked up volume as it echoed off the cathedral ceiling. Most of the congregants turned around in their seats.

Now, everyone knew she was here. Emily's hopes of gaining spiritual uplifting and support from attending the service dimmed but didn't die. Neal really liked Community's new pastor, Joel Blackwell. On Neal's recommendation, Emily was willing to give Community a try despite her past history here. She hadn't meant to trip and knock over the manger scene at the Christmas pageant or make the youth group late to Albany so they'd miss their train to New York for the youth rally.

Emily pasted a smile on her face and nodded to everyone she knew as Mrs. Donnelly escorted her to a seat two pews behind Drew and the blond. He turned and beamed her a smile that almost made Emily drop her hymnal again. She'd have a hard time showing Paradox the new Emily Hazard if she went weak every time he smiled.

From the sermon, she understood her brother's enthusiasm for Pastor Joel. Mrs. Donnelly caught her elbow as she stepped into the aisle to leave after the benediction. "You *are* staying for coffee hour, aren't you? Everyone will want to see you."

Emily wasn't nearly as sure of that as Mrs. Donnelly

seemed to be, nor how anxious she was to see "everyone." She looked around the church for her niece. The pew she'd been in was empty. "I don't know. I need to find Autumn."

"Oh, she and her friends are probably already in the hall. She and Neal always stay, just like your parents did."

But she wasn't like Neal and her parents. That had always been a big part of her problem with fitting in here.

"You haven't met Pastor Joel yet, have you?" Mrs. Donnelly went on to the new subject with barely a breath in between.

"No."

"Well, come along." The older woman moved Emily along into the line filing out of the church.

"Good morning," the jovial minister took Mrs. Donnelly's hand.

"Good morning. This is Emily Hazard, Mary and Ted's daughter."

Emily stared. From a distance, the man was good-looking. Up close he was gorgeous. Drop-dead movie star, rock star gorgeous. And probably not much older than her. She tried not to drool and mentally reminded herself she was in church. All the time she was growing up, they'd never had a pastor under the age of sixty—at least, in her memory.

"Welcome," he said, grasping her hand in both of his. "I was called here just before your parents went to Florida, so I didn't get to know them well, but I've worked with Neal on the church council and Autumn is a great kid."

"Nice to meet you." Emily started to move on.

"And this is my wife, Jennifer."

The blond. Emily hadn't seen her standing on the other side of the minister. She was pretty and petite. A wholesome girl next door pretty.

"Good morning," Jennifer said.

Had she seen Emily drooling over her husband? Her *minister* husband. Emily mumbled something she hoped was appropriate. Most of her wits seemed to have stayed back in the city.

A compatriot sidelined Mrs. Donnelly on their way to the hall. Emily forged ahead alone, skipping the refreshment line and going directly to the coffeepot at the far corner of the room. She poured herself a cup, added a dollop of half-and-half and carried the coffee without mishap—for once—to an empty table at the opposite corner. She scanned the crowd for Autumn. None of the kids from church seemed to be in the hall.

"Hey." Drew placed a plate full of food and a cup of coffee on the table and sat in the chair next to her. "Looking for Autumn so you can make your escape?"

"What gave me away?"

"Could be the desperate glances around the room before and after you sat down along with your gripping the coffee cup as if you were ready to chug it down in one gulp and run."

Heat crept up her neck. How long had he been watching her? And why was she so bothered about it? It wasn't as if she hadn't given him a good once-over when he wasn't looking a time or two over the past few days. His strong features made him more interesting to look at than picture-perfect Pastor Joel. More attractive, actually.

His eyes narrowed at her perusal, and she dropped her gaze to her coffee.

"The youth group leader called an impromptu meeting." He picked up a chocolate brownie that made her stomach growl.

"Autumn said to tell you." He sunk his teeth into the brownie.

She should have braved the line and gotten something to eat.

"You could go back and get one," he said as if reading her mind.

She assessed the line. "No, I'll just have one of yours." She smiled and lifted a chocolate chip cookie from his plate.

"Hey!"

"You didn't get this for me?" She broke the cookie in two and popped half in her mouth. "Mmm."

Drew made a grab for the other half.

She swung her arm back out of his reach and smacked into something hard.

A baby let loose with a wail.

"I'm so sorry."

Emily turned in her chair.

Becca Norton stood to her left holding a baby carrier the size of a small recliner. "I'm such a klutz these days."

Emily stilled.

"It's like I got so used to being pregnant that I can't move normally anymore." Becca lifted the carrier to the table.

Her face was placid giving no hint of the taunt Emily had initially read into her words.

"Who's this big guy?" Drew moved the carrier so that the baby could see both of them.

"Brendon." Becca's face beamed with pride.

The baby tilted his head as if contemplating whether she and Drew were worth his acquaintance and gummed his knuckle.

Becca eyed the cookie in Emily's hand and the goodies on Drew's plate. "Those look really good. But I shouldn't. Still losing the baby weight."

What baby weight? Emily wondered. Becca's simple fitted sheath dress accented the perfect curves the former cheerleader had had since seventh grade, when Emily was still in her chunky stage. Drew's admiring gaze said he was thinking along the same line. She would not acknowledge the comparison Drew must be making by looking down at her less ample figure. Nor did she want to contemplate why she cared.

"Do you mind watching Brendon for me for a minute while I go get a brownie and some tea?"

Watch Brendon? It wasn't as if she and Becca were good friends, and Becca had just met Drew last night. "I was about to—"

"Sure, no problem," Drew said, chucking Brendon under the chin and eliciting a big baby belly laugh in return.

"Yeah, I have to stick around for Autumn." The perverse side of her said she was staying if Drew was staying. She didn't need Becca regaling him with any of the escapades of her high school years. As if they'd have nothing better to talk about except her. She was letting old memories get the best of her.

"Be right back, Button." Becca tickled Brendon's belly and took off for the food line.

Once Becca had moved out of Brendon's sight, he began to fuss.

"Oooo, what's the matter?" Emily cooed. The fussing soon escalated into an all-out cry. She eyed the harness that strapped the baby in the seat. Should she unfasten it and pick him up? Before she could decide, Drew had the straps unsnapped and was swooping Brendon up and over his head.

"What's the matter, big guy? Can't see what's going on?" He held him up high. "That's better, isn't it?"

The howl diminished to a sniffle and, then, to a squeal of delight as Drew swayed him over the table.

Emily's heart warmed. "You're pretty good at that."

"I'm a little out of practice. It's been a while since Mia and Ethan were this small. But this always worked."

"Not as out of practice as me. I can't remember even holding a baby since Autumn."

He nuzzled Brendon. "So your friends haven't joined the mommy train yet?"

"No." Most of the women she worked with didn't have the slightest inclination to have kids, even the ones whose biological clocks were ringing. "There are some young families at church, but I don't really know any of them well."

"Seems like all my friends in the city have caught the baby bug. It's wreaked havoc with my pickup soccer league, not that I'm there to play this season, either." He laughed, but it wasn't enough to completely hide a note of wistfulness.

For the soccer league or the kids? From the way he seemed to be enjoying their impromptu babysitting, she was hard-pressed to decide. Either way he'd fit right in here. Emily couldn't ignore the twinge of jealousy that pricked her. She'd lived here practically her whole life. He'd been here a month.

"I don't imagine Wall Street with a family leaves much time for anything else." She jiggled Brendon's foot and was rewarded with a drooly smile.

"Wall Street *without* a family doesn't leave time for anything else."

Sometimes Emily felt the same about advertising, but the feeling usually went away as quickly as it came. Before she could commiserate, Becca returned with a plate full of cookies. A cupcake perched precariously on top.

"Everything looked so good, I got one of each. Feel free."

The cupcake tumbled off as she placed the plate on the table. It rolled frosting side down onto Drew's lap. Emily pressed her lips together to suppress an uncharitable giggle.

"I'm so sorry." Becca handed Drew a napkin. "Like I said, a klutz. It reminds me of the homecoming game senior year. You remember, Em."

Emily's stomach sank as she rolled back time trying to remember what memorable act she'd committed at homecoming.

"You don't remember? I thought everyone did."

She avoided Drew's curious gaze.

"The squad was doing our pyramid cheer."

She'd done something to disrupt a cheer? That she should

have remembered. She'd rarely gone to any high school games for any sport.

"Matt and Ed Romer. You remember him? He played full-back."

Emily nodded. She'd had a crush on him in seventh grade and made a complete fool of herself over him.

"Well, they were supposed to boost me up to the top to finish the pyramid. I stepped into their joined hands and they boosted me up all right. Up and over the top. I accidentally kicked one of the other girls as I flew over. The whole formation collapsed and I landed on my butt on the other side of the human pile."

Becca was talking about herself? Emily shook her head. "I never heard a word about it."

"You must have been the only one in the student body that didn't."

Emily wanted to feel compassion for Becca. She really did. But that had been one incident for Becca, not a daily occurrence as it had been for Emily.

"I never thought I'd live it down." Becca bit into a brownie as if that might assuage her embarrassment and Emily caught a glimpse of Matt behind her making a beeline for their table.

She closed her eyes for a quick second.

Lord, I know You have more important things, but if You would, please give me the fortitude to survive this conversation if Matt gets over here before Becca finishes and I can change the subject.

"Mmm. These are as good as they looked, which reminds me. We need to get together for lunch." Becca wiped a speck of frosting off her face and laughed. "All I seem to think about these days is food. How about Friday?"

Emily had hoped Becca was making polite conversation when she'd suggested lunch at the VFW party.

"Friday's fine."

"Noon at the diner? I'll have to bring Brendon. They're set up for kids there."

The baby gurgled at the sound of his name and Drew tickled his belly again. He really seemed to like kids.

"The diner is fine."

"Hey, babe, ready?" Matt reached their table and picked up Brendon and the baby carrier. "Jinx, Drew." He nodded to them. "How's it going?" His smile was so genuine that Emily didn't even cringe much at the use of her nickname. "I'll go ahead and get him settled in the car. We're supposed to be at Mom's for dinner at two, and this guy needs a nap first."

"More food. Great." Becca grinned.

Matt shook his head at Becca. "Later." He nodded at Emily and Drew.

"I'll see you Friday," Becca said.

"I've got to get going, too," Drew said. "I've got a load of materials being delivered."

"On Sunday?"

"Yep. I usually don't work on Sunday, but we're behind on some of the outdoor work because of all the rain we've had the past couple of weeks. Don't worry about dinner. I'll swing by the diner and pick up a pizza for the three of us if that's okay."

"Sure." She'd planned to catch up on her campaign work and hadn't given a thought to Sunday dinner. Guilt pricked her. Her mother had always liked them all there for Sunday dinner. Autumn was probably expecting a family dinner, too.

Drew wondered if Emily had any idea how expressive her face and body language was. The wide-eyed look of horror when Becca asked if they'd watch Brendon while she got food. The tension that radiated from her when Becca started talking about the high school game. The way her eyes lit up when he said he'd bring dinner.

"Good morning."

Drew recognized the older man who was entering the church hall as he was leaving, but he couldn't remember his name. Then again, the way Emily was occupying his thoughts was making it hard to remember much of anything.

"Pastor Joel did it again," the man said. "Another on-point sermon."

"Certainly was." Drew wasn't lying, even though he wasn't sure what Joel had said. His mind had kept drifting back to a picture of Mrs. Donnelly dragging a reluctant Emily up the church aisle to sit behind him. It had taken all his concentration to not turn around and check whether she'd been staring at him or he'd only imagined her gaze boring down on him and Jennifer.

"You're the young man who's fixing up the lodge at the Hazard's campground, aren't you?"

"Yes, I am."

"We had some good times there." The man regaled him with stories of summers past until Drew feared he'd miss his lumber store delivery.

He took advantage of a brief lull when the man stopped to take a breath. "I'd better get going. I have a truckload of building materials coming."

"On Sunday?" he asked just as Emily had, but with a deep tone of disapproval.

"I wouldn't if I didn't have to get everything done before the campers arrive. Why don't you stop over this week and see how the lodge is coming?"

"I'll do that," the man said, all disapproval gone. "I hear Jinx is home. I can stop in and say hello to her, too. I was her elementary school principal. She was one of my favorites. So inquisitive about everything. Never walked when she could run."

Great, now he had visions of a pint-sized Jinx filling the spaces in his head that weren't already filled with images of the grown Emily. He was in big trouble.

* * *

Emily picked up her plate and napkin and started toward the trash bin. Drew stood in the doorway across the hall talking with her elementary school principal. Two women she didn't know were smiling in his direction and talking to each other. She crushed the plate and continued her trek.

"Here you are." Autumn headed her off at the bin. "I thought you'd be outside waiting for me."

A tap on the shoulder turned Emily's attention away from her niece. Another of her mother's friends said how good it was to see her, warming her heart. For someone who never fit in, she sure seemed to be getting a warm welcome back.

"If you're done socializing, I'd like to go." Autumn stood, hands on hips.

As if her likes and dislikes reigned supreme. Emily was very tempted to go get another coffee. But that would be as childish as Autumn was acting. And Autumn was the child.

"I've got to get home and finish the research for my economics paper."

Emily dropped her trash in the bin. "I thought you and Jack were going to study together this afternoon." She hadn't questioned how that was going to work, with Autumn still in high school and Jack at community college.

"So did I. But one of his friends' car broke down and he's going over to help him fix it. Who knows how long that will take." She rolled her eyes as if it were all too much to take.

That explained the foul mood. "So, what's your paper about?"

Autumn made a face. "An analysis of economic policy in the U.S. leading up to the Great Depression. We didn't even get to choose our own topic. The teacher gave us a choice of five. For a class of twenty-five. I told you he was lame."

"Well, you don't have too much longer until the class is over."

"There is that. What are you doing today?"

"I was going to work on my ad campaign this afternoon." But she could change her plans if Autumn wanted to do something with her. "Drew's up at the lodge. He's going to pick up pizza at the diner for dinner."

"From the diner? Have you had pizza from the diner?"

"Not recently. But I'm happy to not have to cook. If you'd like, I can call Drew and tell him not to bother."

"And make me cook? Remember, I've had your cooking."

Although Emily would be the first to admit she was no chef, her niece's criticism grated.

Autumn cranked the sound up on the radio as soon as they got in the SUV and Emily gripped the steering wheel tight to resist turning it down. Autumn's attitude was pushing her to the edge. Emily was only twenty-six. She would not turn into her mother. At least not yet. Maybe Becca could give her some insight. She worked with kids. And Drew. A replay of him with Brendon ran through Emily's mind and she smiled to herself. Although his experience with older kids was limited to boys.

When they got home, Emily grabbed a container of her favorite yogurt and a clementine orange from the refrigerator for lunch. She smiled. It looked like Neal had stocked up on all of her favorites. Opening the cupboard to find chocolate-dipped Oreos confirmed it.

"I'm going to get to work." *After I call Mom and ask her what to do with you.*

Autumn looked at her. Surely, she wasn't expecting her to make her lunch. Neal couldn't pamper her that much. And she *had* grown up with Emily's mother living here, although that hadn't done much to hone Emily's culinary skills. She crossed the kitchen to the archway into the living room.

"I guess I'll make a sandwich." Autumn sighed.

Autumn was going to have to realize who was in charge here. Emily definitely had her work cut out for her.

* * *

Emily shut down her computer. She'd been working all afternoon and had accomplished next to nothing. She went to the kitchen and picked up the phone and punched in the number. "Hey, Mom."

"Ji—Emily!"

She smiled at her mother's correction.

"I was thinking about you this morning at church," her mom continued.

"When you should have been listening to the sermon?"

"You've got me there. I miss Community. Neal couldn't say enough good about Pastor Joel when he was down here visiting."

"To me, too."

"But I'm sure you're not calling about church. Autumn?"

"Yeah."

"She's a handful. And troubled about something. I noticed that when they were visiting."

"Oh, good." She stopped pacing the room and sat.

"Good?"

"I didn't mean that. But I was starting to think it was me and that I was looking at a rough couple months ahead. I hadn't realized how little I've seen her since I moved to New York. I hardly know her anymore."

"It'll take a bit to get into a routine, but you'll do fine."

"You don't know what's bothering her aside from Neal being called up?"

"Not really. She's always been a little self-centered. Neal spoils her. He never got past the 'poor little motherless baby.' Without your dad and me there, I'll bet she's been running the household."

"But, Mom, what teen isn't self-centered?"

"It's gotten worse. In a lot of ways she's immature for her age. You'd outgrown most of that nonsense by the time you were sixteen."

Didn't her mother realize that she had lived a totally different high school life than Autumn who, from what she could tell, was one of the popular kids at school?

"And she's way too much into all those internet social network things."

Emily swallowed a groan. Not the computer again.

"I'll bet Neal let her move the computer into her room."

She didn't have the heart to tell her he'd gone one step further and bought Autumn a laptop and set up a wireless network so she could use it anywhere she wanted.

"So what do I do? How do I find out what's going on with her? We haven't gotten off to a great start."

An audible sigh passed over the phone lines. "She's been talking with Mrs. Edwards, you know. A lot, I think. That woman even called her here when Autumn and Neal were visiting for Easter."

No, she didn't know Autumn had been talking with her other grandmother. Nor did that seem particularly relevant. Her mother had never liked Audrey Edwards, not even enough to be on a first-name basis. "Understandable. She's probably encouraging Autumn to reconsider Trinity for the fall. After all, her grandfather got her in the early enrollment program. She could have started in January."

"He didn't get her in. Her grades did."

She ignored her mother's correction. "I give them credit for being able to get her to apply. She's so entrenched here in Paradox. It wouldn't hurt her to see some more of the world."

"There's nothing wrong with her wanting to stay in Paradox."

"You guys didn't." Emily could have cut her tongue for letting that slip out.

"Emily Eve Hazard."

Her full name. She was in trouble.

"You know full well the only reason we came down here

to stay with your grandmother was so she didn't have to go into a nursing home after her stroke.

Emily scuffed her toe. "I know. I'm sorry."

"We don't plan to stay here permanently."

Somehow she wasn't surprised that her parents would give up Grandma's town house in sunny Florida for Northern New York, where you could experience all four seasons in one week. Not that she could even begin to understand their reasoning.

"But, you've given Neal the house and the campground."

"No. We still own the house. Neal bought a half interest in the campground, with an option to buy the other half. Of course, if you're interested in the other half..." Her mother's voice trailed off.

"Thanks, but no thanks." She softened her tone. "I don't have the time to be involved with the campground. I can come visit Neal any time I need a dose of wilderness." Which wasn't often, but she didn't need to tell Mom that.

Her father's voice rumbled in the background, as if in response to her thought.

"Your dad wants to know how the lodge is shaping up."

"I don't know. I haven't been over yet."

Her mother relayed that information to her father. "Drew seems like a good guy and so responsible, taking on all the work of setting up and running the summer camp. He's not much older than you, you know, and he's from New York."

First Autumn, then Neal and now her mother was matchmaking. She should be irritated, but she was more amused. "You've met him?"

"No. We've talked with him on the phone a couple of times, but not nearly enough for your father. He'd like day-by-day or, even better, hour-by-hour updates on the renovations."

"He's that bored?"

"Pretty much. I'm busy with your grandmother. She prefers me to take care of her, even though he's more than willing to. He doesn't golf. I keep telling him to use the pool. You know how he likes to swim. Of course, he compares the pool to the lake, and you know which one comes out ahead."

"No question there." Her dad always joked that he had lake water in his veins. "What about church?"

"He's trying to get involved. But it's different, not knowing everyone. The congregation is so big, a little impersonal."

More like her church in New York. "You could try out some others."

"No, Mom likes this one when she feels up to going. Your dad will be fine as soon as he gets to know some of the people better."

A commotion in the background on her mother's end interrupted the conversation.

"That's your grandmother. She wants to get up. I'd better go help her."

"Sure. Bye." She hung up realizing that she wasn't any further ahead with figuring out Autumn than she'd been before she'd made the call. As she reached to return the receiver to the charger, she noticed the voice mail indicator flashing.

A thud on the door to the garage stopped her from retrieving the message. Probably Jack. She turned and saw Drew through the window. Why was he knocking? Because she'd complained about Jack walking in? She opened the door.

"Pizza delivery." Drew stood on the steps with two pizza boxes and a gallon of iced tea in hand. "Sorry about the kick at the door. My hands were full."

"I never find fault with people bringing food I don't have to cook." She took the jug of tea from him with her free hand. "How much do I owe you?"

He placed the pizzas on the counter. "My treat."

She eyed the boxes.

"They were buy one, get one half price. I can take the extra for lunch."

She held up the phone. "Let me check the voice mail and go get Autumn." She entered the phone number and password.

It was Mrs. Edwards. "Autumn, it's Nana. I have more information for you. Please call back." Emily turned the phone off. More information? Maybe it was about Trinity. Could Autumn be considering going there in the fall after all? It would explain the phone calls Mom had mentioned and, possibly, Autumn's behavior—or at least part of it.

She walked through the living room to the bottom of the stairway. "Autumn, pizza."

The muffled response sounded like an affirmative and the click of the door opening confirmed it.

When she returned to the kitchen, Drew had set the table with cups, forks and napkins. A stack of paper plates sat on the counter. The fact that he knew his way around the kitchen so well, probably better than she did, made her a little uneasy.

Autumn sauntered in and lifted the lids on the pizzas. "Good. You didn't ruin them with anchovies like Daddy does. He only has them put them on half, but I can still taste them on my pieces."

Emily joined her niece at the counter. "Double meat and veggies. How did you know?" She picked up a plate and piled on a couple of pieces.

"I could say you seem like a meat and veggies kind of girl, but actually it's my favorite."

"Great minds." They shared a smile.

Autumn wrinkled her nose at them, put a couple of pieces of pizza on a plate, and went to the table. She sat and began picking the peppers off. Emily sat across from her and Drew took the chair between them.

"There's a voice mail message for you from your nana," Emily said before she bit into her pizza.

Autumn's eyes widened as she looked at her over the top of her glass of tea. "What did she say?"

"Something about having information for you."

"Oh." Autumn took a gulp of tea.

"Could be what you're waiting for," Drew said.

What did he know that she didn't and why?

"I'll call her back later." Autumn set her tea down.

"Is it about college?"

"No." Autumn pushed the peppers around her plate with the point of her pizza. "Daddy didn't tell you?"

Neal hadn't told her a lot of things, apparently.

Drew and Autumn exchanged a glance, and he nodded almost imperceptivity.

The bite of pizza Emily had taken turned to soggy cardboard in her mouth. Drew was giving Autumn the go-ahead to talk to her.

"Nana hired a private investigator."

Not again. Mrs. Edwards had hired private eyes to try to find Autumn's mother in the past, too many times to count. But not, to her knowledge, since Autumn had been old enough to be privy to the investigation.

"Don't say anything. I can tell by your face what you're thinking. This time the investigator thinks he has a solid lead."

"You knew about the other times?"

Autumn shrugged. "Some of them. I was a kid, not blind and deaf. I'd listen to Dad talk to Nana."

She caught Drew looking past her to the door. "Maybe we should talk about this later."

"Drew knows. More than you do."

Neal must have had his reasons for sharing this with Drew.

"Stay." It was selfish of her to ask, but Drew would be a welcome buffer between her and Autumn.

Autumn folded her paper plate over her unfinished pizza.

She walked to the trash container and dropped it in. "I'm going to go call Nana."

Emily opened her mouth to stop her, find out more.

Drew placed his hand on hers, warm and strong, and her agitation subsided.

"Let her go."

"I didn't know. It explains why she's so prickly."

"Neal didn't want to forbid her from talking with her grandmother."

"Of course not." Mrs. Edwards made no secret that one of her fondest wishes was to reunite Autumn and her mother, Vanessa, if they ever found her. The sentiment was good, but no way could Emily see any good in setting Autumn up with unrealistic expectations.

"I know he's been praying for direction."

She bit her lip. It was hard for her to imagine Neal being so public with someone he'd known such a short time. Pastor Joel, yes. But Drew?

"Why you?" The words were out before she realized she'd said them out loud.

He shrugged. "I was here. I'm a good listener. He was drowning in his responsibilities. Raising a kid alone is hard."

Emily bit her lip. Drew might be good with kids and coach soccer, but he didn't actually have any kids of his own.

He drummed his fingers on the table. "My mom raised my brother and me by herself. Of course, as a kid, I had no appreciation of all she did for us."

So that's where his voice of experience came from. Why was she so quick to shoot him down?

Drew reached across and lifted her chin.

The tremor that went through her answered her question. To diminish the attraction she was in danger of giving into.

He held her gaze. "We could double-team her. My experience with teenage boy soccer players and yours with persnickety clients and temperamental artists. What better qualifications for handling a sullen teenage girl?"

"Sure. Sounds like a plan."

Although right now it seemed more like a recipe for disaster.

Chapter Six

As her mom had said they would, by the end of the week, Emily and Autumn and Drew were getting into a routine. Much to Emily's surprise, Autumn had taken on making dinner. The teen said that was her deal with her dad. She cooked, and Neal cleaned up. Emily was all for letting her continue since Autumn's cooking skills, it turned out, far surpassed hers. And Drew had pitched in on the cleanup, which made quick work of it. She and Autumn had even discovered that they liked a couple of the same TV shows.

Her niece had been silent about whatever information her grandmother had called with on Sunday. Emily hadn't pushed it. She'd had enough conflict with work not to go looking for more in her personal life. The transition to telecommuting had not gone anywhere near as smoothly as she'd hoped. The few changes the client had sent at the end of last week had turned into a total redo. After working ten-hour days Monday through Thursday, with half of that time on the phone with her boss or the client—or so it seemed—she finally had the new proposal ready.

Emily put the drawing stylus in its holder and stared at the dark clouds moving across the late morning sky. She was actually looking forward to lunch with Becca, even if it meant braving an Adirondack thunderstorm to get there. The phone rang as she stood to go get ready. She groaned when she checked the caller ID and saw her office number.

"Emily," her boss Donna started without any greeting. "You've got to get down here. My client is about to pull their campaign."

"What's the problem?" She might have been more concerned if the art director didn't say this whenever a client contacted her with anything that could be remotely construed as a complaint.

"Bob isn't comfortable viewing your digital presentation. He wants an in person one."

Emily gritted her teeth. He might have mentioned that during one of the seven times they'd talked on the phone this week. "Okay, I'll send you the presentation this morning and you can have someone print up the art boards."

"But it's your presentation. No one else has worked on it."

She should appreciate that the art director thought she was the only one who could make the presentation. But in reality, the campaign wasn't that unique and the printed art boards would be pretty self-explanatory. Besides, Bob had already seen and approved the digital roughs she'd sent him Wednesday night.

"I figured you couldn't get down here today, could you?"

Was she kidding? "No."

"Yeah, that's what I thought, so I set the meeting for tomorrow at one."

"What?"

"You can send me the digital presentation and I'll have someone work up the boards for you. It's what, a four-hour drive? We'll have an early lunch, and you can brainstorm your concepts with me."

Emily held her temper. She had been the one who had insisted she could do her job long-distance, that Paradox wasn't that far from New York City, that she could come down periodically if she needed to. But she hadn't even been gone a week.

"Emily, are you still there?"

"Yes. There must have been a blip in the reception."

"All right. Then, I'll see you at the office about eleven tomorrow morning."

She stared at the buzzing phone. Donna had hung up before she could get another word out. Before she could return the phone to the holder, it rang again. What did she want now? For her to whip up an alternate campaign this afternoon in case Bob didn't like the one he'd already approved? But it wasn't Donna. It was a local number.

"Hello?"

"Emily, it's Becca. I'm really sorry, I have to reschedule our lunch. Brendon's running a fever this morning."

"Is he okay?"

"He's probably just teething, but I'd rather not take him out."

"Oh sure. I understand."

"I'm going to be down in North Carolina visiting my mom next week. You know Dad took a transfer there after my brother graduated high school."

People kept saying that, but actually she didn't know. Probably, she thought with a twinge of guilt, because she hadn't paid attention when her mother had told her.

"I'll give you a call after I get back. Any day better for you?"

"No, any day is fine." Did that sound as desperate to Becca as it sounded to her?

Brendon yowled in the background. "I've got to go. I really am sorry. Talk with you later."

Emily returned to the computer and tapped the stylus against the drawing pad. Strangely, she was more disappointed about Becca canceling their lunch than she was looking forward to her strategy session with Donna tomorrow morning, which confused her. She and Donna were a good team. She wanted to *be* Donna someday.

"You know that works better if you turn the computer on."

She spun the chair around.

Drew stood in the doorway grinning. "I'm headed down to Glens Falls for some plumbing stuff. I've got a break in one of the water pipes at the lodge. So count me out for dinner."

"You have a broken pipe and you're still smiling?"

"What can I say? I like the view."

She reached down and pressed the computer's on button to hide how his compliment unsettled her.

"Do you need anything?"

"No, not that I can think of." She righted herself. "But I do need a favor. Are you going to be around this weekend?"

"Tonight. I'm going to my mom's tomorrow afternoon. Sunday is her birthday. Why?"

"My boss just called. I've got to go down to the city for a client meeting and I was hoping not to have to rush right back tomorrow evening. I don't want to leave Autumn alone overnight."

"We can go down together."

Four hours alone in the truck with Drew. Her pulse quickened. Not a good idea. But Autumn would be with them.

"Mom won't mind the extra company."

"I don't want to put your mother out. Autumn and I will stay at a hotel."

"Believe me. You wouldn't be putting her out. She was always after Scott and me to bring our friends home."

A ripple of pleasure rolled through her at his referring to her as a friend. "If you're sure."

"I'm sure."

"It might be fun. Autumn hasn't been to New York before. If my meeting doesn't last too long, I can show her around

New York and meet you at your mother's later. Give you some time with her before we arrive."

"Oh, I don't know. Sometimes there's safety in numbers."

The late bus brought Autumn home from softball practice, and, as usual, she went right to work on dinner. Emily told her about the weekend in New York.

"But I have plans for tomorrow night."

What plans could Autumn have that were better than a trip to New York?

"Jack and Jule, and Ezra and I have tickets to see Carrie Underwood at the Glens Falls Civic Center."

A concert with friends would definitely have more allure for a seventeen-year-old than a weekend trip to New York with an aunt, especially since she'd be spending a good part of the time working.

"I don't like leaving you alone."

"I won't be alone. I'll be with my friends." Autumn turned from the salad greens she was tearing into a bowl and stood feet apart, hands on hips. "You don't trust me."

"It's not—" Emily stopped herself. But it was. No sense lying about it. "I'm uncomfortable with my being so far away. The house is pretty secluded."

"So, I'll have Jule stay over."

And Jack and Ezra.

Autumn's eye narrowed. "I know what you're thinking. So how's it fine that you and Drew go off to New York alone and it's not fine if I stay here with Jule?"

Her and Drew? "It's not like that. We're not… I don't…" She could kick herself for letting Autumn turn things around so that she felt she was the teenager and Autumn was the adult.

"I don't, either." Autumn stomped off toward her room.

Emily gave her a few minutes. Then she went upstairs and knocked on her door. "Can I come in?"

"Do I have a choice?" Autumn pulled the door open.

Deep breath. "I don't have to stay over in New York. I can take the truck, drive back after my meeting and be here when you get home from the concert."

"Whoopee! But don't put yourself out for me. I'll stay over at Jule's. Mrs. Hill can babysit me for you." She flounced away from Emily. "You know Dad and the Hills think we're old enough to get our own apartment in Ticonderoga for college in a couple months. You don't think I'm old enough to stay alone for one day."

"That's in a couple months. This is now. Your father asked me to come and stay here with you. If he'd wanted me to supervise you from New York, he would have said that. It would have been a lot easier for me to stay in my apartment, and not try to do my job from 250 miles away."

Autumn stooped down and picked up a crumpled paper from the floor and tossed it across the room at the wastebasket. It went in with a soft rustle. "Sorry."

"Accepted. I'll go call Mrs. Hill to make sure it's no problem and then, I'll finish fixing dinner."

"Do you have to?"

"I'm hungry and even my cooking is better than none."

"No, I mean call Mrs. Hill."

"Yes, I do."

"You're as bad as Grandma."

"I'll take that as a compliment."

Autumn sighed and plopped onto the bed. "But you're only twenty-six."

Emily pushed back a strand of hair that had strayed from her braid. She felt ninety-six. "I'll give you a shout if the salad gets the best of me."

"You are going to wait and let Drew grill the burgers,

right?" She placed her feet on the floor as if she were going to stand.

"Can't. He's gone to Glens Falls." Emily turned to leave.

"Aunt Jinx?"

She stopped and turned back to catch Autumn brushing the corner of one eye with her finger.

"I really am sorry."

"I know. But I really have to be the bad guy until your dad comes home. Then, maybe I can get you down to New York for a girls' weekend. Deal?"

"Deal. And I'll be down in a minute to handle the grill."

Emily shut the door behind her and leaned against the wall for a moment. How did parents do this day in and day out, year after year? She should send Mom a big bouquet of the yellow roses she loved, just because.

Drew paused at the door. Emily sat at the kitchen table, her back to him, sipping coffee. The early morning sun caught the lighter streaks in her honey-brown hair. She had it all wound up in the back giving him a view of the graceful curve of her neck above the soft collar of her blue shirt.

"Got any more of that?"

She turned in the chair and smiled, stopping him midstep. "Maybe. What's in it for me?"

"There is my offer of a ride down to the city."

"Sounds fair to me."

He walked around her to the coffeemaker and poured a cup. "You and Autumn manage the grill okay last night without me?"

She nodded, looking at him over the rim of her coffee cup. Or, at least he thought she was. She could have been checking the time on the clock behind him. No, she was looking at him.

"I won't make any claims to managing. Autumn knew all

about firing it up, and grilling the burgers. Did you get the water break at the lodge fixed?"

"Should be. But I left the water shut off. I'll check it Monday." He'd be more confident of his work if thoughts of him and her alone in his truck for four hours hadn't been rushing through his mind the whole time he'd been repairing the pipes.

Drew sat across from Emily and added a scoop of sugar to his coffee, then pushed back from the table. He'd forgotten to get a teaspoon. She handed him hers. He wasn't even going to acknowledge the charge that small gesture set off. All she did was hand him a spoon. A spoon she'd already used to stir her coffee. Coffee that had cream in it. He never used cream.

"Ah, thanks." He glanced toward the living room. "Autumn had better get a move on it. I want to get a breakfast sandwich at the corner store on our way."

"Autumn isn't coming. She and Jack and Jule and some other friend have tickets to a concert tonight in Glens Falls."

"You're leaving her here by herself for the weekend? Not a good idea."

She put her coffee mug down. "I know. I talked with Mrs. Hill last night. She said it would be no problem for Autumn to stay there with Jule."

"That's my girl." It just slipped out. He searched her eyes for a reaction. They widened slightly, but she didn't acknowledge his unintended endearment. He loosened the death grip he had on his coffee mug.

"Autumn didn't think it was so great an idea, but she got over it." Emily rose and went to the sink to wash out her cup.

He gulped down the rest of his coffee and did the same.

"Time to get going. Where's your bag?"

"By the door."

He grabbed both her overnight case and laptop and loaded them in the backseat of his truck along with his sports bag.

They climbed in his truck and started down the driveway.

"Stop." She grabbed his leg as the truck approached the road.

His pulse quickened. That dull thump had been a rock in the drive. He couldn't have hit a squirrel or something. He hadn't seen anything. Still didn't see anything in their path.

"I think I forgot my thumb drive with the presentation." She opened the door and jumped out before he brought the vehicle to a full stop. Didn't she know she could kill herself doing that?

Watching her race up the driveway in her flimsy little dress sandals didn't do anything to calm his racing heart. She was an accident waiting to happen. And much as he might like to be, he wasn't the white knight she needed to rescue her. Not until he got his life sorted out, at least. He turned the truck off and breathed in and out evenly, choosing not to watch her race back to the truck.

"Got it."

He turned the ignition.

"Wait."

"What?"

"I don't know if I have my cell phone." She dug through her purse and held it up triumphantly when she found it.

He'd like to think that he had a part in throwing off her equilibrium, and this wasn't simply the Jinx side of Emily.

"Got everything?"

She touched the screen of her phone and read down a list. "Yes. I should have double-checked before we left the house."

He swung the pickup into the convenience store at the crossroads in town and she tilted her head in question. A faint scent of flowers tickled his nostrils.

"Do you need gas?" She reached for her purse. "I can write off the trip. Business."

Her offer irritated him. He didn't want to be just business. "The tank's full. I'm going to get a breakfast sandwich. Want one?"

She wrinkled her nose emphasizing the sprinkle of freckles that peeked through her carefully applied makeup. His irritation faded.

"Or a coffee?"

"No, thanks. I've had enough coffee and I had a granola bar with my first cup."

"Be right back."

Mike, the owner, greeted him as he entered the store. "Hey there. The usual?"

"Yep, and make the coffee a large."

"Tough day ahead?"

"Possibly." He glanced out the window at Emily who appeared to be writing something on her lap. "Very possibly." He settled up and took the paper-wrapped sandwich and coffee cup.

Emily opened her door when she saw him. "Want me to drive while you eat that?"

He didn't let anyone drive his truck. Especially anyone nicknamed Jinx.

"I've been driving pickups since I was sixteen."

Not his pickup. "No problem. I always eat my breakfast on my way to work at the lodge. Finish up whatever you were working on." He motioned at a sketchbook on the seat next to her.

"If you're sure."

"I'm sure." He slid behind the steering wheel, put his coffee in the cup holder and peeled the wrapper off his sandwich.

"That does smell good."

He stopped prebite. "Last chance if you want one."

She placed her hand on her flat stomach. "No, I'll enjoy yours vicariously. I have to leave room for my early lunch with my boss."

Drew finished his bite, savoring the spicy tang of the convenience store's own sausage and local cheddar cheese. He washed it down with coffee and started the truck. "Mind if I turn the radio on?"

"Go ahead." She bent over the pad and went back to work on whatever she'd started when he was in the store.

He finished his sandwich and tapped his finger against the steering wheel in time to the music on the radio until they reached the Northway south to Albany and New York. "What are you working on?"

She looked up from the pad, her gray eyes bright. "I had the best idea for jazzing up my presentation when you were in the store. I've sketched it out." She held the pad out to him.

The car on their right honked as the truck veered slightly in that direction. He turned his attention back to the road. "Tell me about it."

She lowered the pad. "I could run through the presentation. Without the visuals." She glanced out her window at the car beside them. "If you don't mind."

"Not at all." This might be interesting, seeing Emily at work.

"You're going to have to visualize the art boards to go with my talk." She described the boards with the new spin she'd come up with before she launched into the presentation complete with the appropriate gestures toward the imaginary art board.

"So, what did you think?" she asked after her close.

"I'm sold." The idea was clever and her makeshift presentation had been flawless, from what he could tell. Then again, he might have simply been enjoying her enthusiasm.

"Thanks. You don't think it's too out there?"

"No, and I'll bet it's even better with the visuals."

She punched him playfully in the arm.

"Seriously, I'd like to see your artwork."

She reached over the seat back for her laptop.

"But not right now. I'm driving."

She laughed. "Don't worry. I won't distract you."

A little late for that. He'd been distracted since she arrived in Paradox.

She flipped the computer open and booted it. "I'm going to tweak my files to reflect the changes I sketched out. Hope you don't mind. I probably won't be much company for the rest of the trip."

"It's work. I understand." He stretched his leg, repositioned himself in his seat and ignored that simply having her seated beside him was company enough.

Chapter Seven

Emily pulled open the plate glass door and a familiar rush of adrenaline shot through her. The elevator couldn't get her up to the fourth floor fast enough.

She walked through the empty reception area with its six-foot tall windows and accents of bright oranges and reds and poked her head in Donna's office. "Wait until you see what I came up with on the drive down. Bob is going to love it."

"He already does."

"I know he liked the prelims." She placed her laptop on her boss's desk and turned it on.

"He liked the presentation."

What was she talking about? He hadn't seen the presentation. That's why she was here.

Donna swung toward her in her chair and crossed her legs. "Change of plans. With the unseasonably warm weather forecasted for today, Bob wanted to get in a round of golf this afternoon. He rescheduled for this morning."

"What? Why didn't you call me?" She grasped the edge of the desk. "Remember, on the phone, I suggested you could have someone else make the presentation."

"I didn't want to disappoint you. You've been gone a week.

I knew you must be dying to get out of Podunk, and I didn't want to take away your reason."

So her whole confrontation with Autumn had been unnecessary. Emily slumped in the chair beside Donna's desk. "So you met with Bob."

"I did. And Amy."

Amy. The recent Rhode Island School of Design grad who'd set herself up as Emily's biggest rival. Her fingers curved inward toward her palms. Amy was the last person she'd had in mind for making her presentation.

"I had her do the presentation from your notes."

Her nails dug into her palms.

"Nice job, by the way."

"Thanks. Bob had pretty much approved it all over the phone."

Donna leaned back in her chair. "About that. Bob is put off by having to work with you long-distance by phone."

"We've always worked over the phone." How was talking to him on the phone from Paradox any different than talking to him on the phone from the office?

Her boss shrugged. "All I can tell you is what he said. He and Amy hit it off, so I've put her on the campaign."

Emily swallowed the bile that rose in her throat. "I've worked with Bob for the past three years."

"You know clients can be fickle, and they're always right." Donna flashed a smile that Emily knew from experience was totally false. "Hey, don't look so worried. I have something better for you."

"I was a little worried. About the work flow. You didn't have me conference in on the production meeting yesterday." Emily and Donna and the agency's two executive partners always went over the new jobs on Friday afternoon so Emily could schedule the work flow for the next week.

"You had to get ready to come down today. I didn't want to add that."

"So you had Amy sit in."

"Never. She was too busy putting the final touches on the art boards you sent."

Emily stretched and flexed her fingers. All of the final touches had been added to the art boards before she sent them. "I see."

"You can't be mad. You said yourself that you had tweaked your files on the drive down."

"True." She folded her hands and rubbed one thumb around the other.

"Wait until you see this job. It's a cream puff. I've got the notes from the meeting right here." She handed Emily a folder. "See what you can work up, and we'll talk about it before I put you in touch with the client."

Emily flipped through the folder. It was a depressingly minor job for a small regional clothing distributor.

"Isn't it perfect? Hiking gear. And you up there in the great outdoors with all those hiking trails and stuff."

She didn't get the connection. Donna knew she wasn't the outdoors type. But it was work. She tucked the file in her bag. "About the production meeting. Do you want to give me the rest of the notes so I can work up the schedule over the weekend?" Not that that was how she wanted to spend her time.

"Don't worry. I assigned the new jobs and gave the notes to the receptionist to add to the production schedule."

The receptionist was a temp. Donna probably didn't even know her name. Didn't she have any idea of how much time and effort she'd put into those schedules? "I'd like to be included in next week's meeting as usual."

Donna stiffened at her tone. "Oh. Of course. I thought I was doing you a favor."

"It puts me at a disadvantage not to know what's going on."

The false smile came out again. "This place is nuts."

Donna spread her hands palms up. "Who ever knows what's going on here?"

Emily liked to think she did, at least when she came into the office every day.

"Now, back to the great outdoors."

Emily reached in her bag to get the folder out again. Donna must have changed her mind about waiting until she'd worked up some ideas before they talked about the job.

"Tell me all about that mountain man you're rooming with."

Emily flushed. "He's not a mountain man, and he's not rooming with me."

"Sor-ry! He is staying at your brother's house. And whatever he is brought a nice blush to your cheeks."

"I don't suppose I can blame it on the heat."

"No. Spill."

"He used to work on Wall Street and is acting as director of a church camp for the summer. Sort of a favor for his brother who's a minister in Brooklyn."

"Good, good. You're into that religious stuff, aren't you?"

"I wouldn't put it exactly that way. I belong to a church. Lots of people do." She picked a nonexistent piece of lint from her slacks. She didn't know why she let Donna put her on the defensive. She was a Christian and should have said so.

"What's he look like?"

She pictured him sitting across the table from her this morning. "You know that dark-haired soccer player in the Simon Stahl commercial we produced. Like that, but better."

"Get out! What are you doing sitting around here with me? Get thee back to the mountains."

"As it happens, I've brought him with me." Donna didn't have to know that he was going to his mother's for her birthday anyway, and that they were staying with her.

"Is he picking you up? Can I get a peek?"

"No. I told him I'd meet him at…uh…his place after the meeting."

Donna banged the desktop with her coffee cup as if it were a gavel. "I declare our meeting officially over. Go," she commanded.

Emily stood. "I'll talk to you Monday."

"Yeah, I'll want to know all about your weekend."

Emily had meant about the project. Why had she let Donna think that she and Drew were an item? They'd only known each other a week and it wasn't like he'd shown any interest—even if she was interested. Which she wasn't. Well, not really interested. They were friends. New friends.

In the elevator, she said a quick prayer asking for forgiveness for her lies of omission. If that's what they were. All she knew was that she didn't feel good about her conversation with her boss.

Her stomach rumbled as she stepped off the elevator. Donna hadn't delivered on the promised lunch. That went right along with giving Amy the campaign for one of the agency's biggest clients. Her client.

She grabbed a hot dog and soda from one of the street vendors and hopped the subway to Brooklyn, exiting at the Bergen Street station. Neat brownstones with wide stone staircases and wrought iron railings lined both sides of the street. She spotted Drew's truck and walked in that direction, checking the house numbers for six hundred. His truck was in front of five-ninety-four. She walked on past two more addresses, her heart beating faster with each step.

The black script on the brick wall said six hundred. She pulled the paper with the address on it from the pocket of her slacks to make sure. While the Jinx side of her usually stayed in the mountains, she couldn't be too sure and didn't want to go knocking on some stranger's door. Although that's what she was doing. She didn't know Drew's mother, didn't really know him that well. A wave of nervousness rippled through her. Now she was being silly. She shoved the paper back into her pocket, marched up the stairs and pushed the buzzer.

"Yes," a high-pitched, but not unpleasant voice came across the intercom.

"Miz Stacey?" She blended Ms. and Mrs. together since she didn't know which address Drew's mother preferred. "It's Emily Hazard…Drew's friend." Following the click of the dead bolt and rustle of a chain, the stained oak door opened inward.

"Come in. Call me Terry," the trim dark-haired woman said. She motioned her into the room. "Drew wasn't expecting you until later. He's down at the field watching his soccer team play."

"Sorry to be so early. My meeting didn't last as long as I thought it would."

"Sit down. Do you want a drink? Water? Tea?" Terry started off toward the opposite doorway.

"Tea would be nice." She sat on the well-worn sofa. The room was beautiful with a high ceiling and light hardwood floors. And large. It dwarfed the simple living room set.

Terry returned a few minutes later and placed a wooden tray with a yellow teapot and two matching mugs on the coffee table. She filled the mugs.

"Drew tells me you're an artist here in the city, when you're not taking care of your niece." She sat in the side chair next to the sofa.

"I'm in advertising in Manhattan. I'm telecommuting while I'm in Paradox. And what do you do?" Terry Stacey looked far too young to be retired. But from what she'd seen of the house, maybe she didn't have to work.

"I work in the City Controller's office."

"So Drew got his math abilities from you."

Terry looked at her blankly.

"He was an analyst on Wall Street."

"Oh, no. I'm just a clerk. He certainly didn't get his math skills from me."

They both picked up their mugs and took a sip. The sweet hot liquid did little to wash away the heavy silence.

Emily tapped her fingernail against the mug. "You have a beautiful home."

"Would you like to see the rest of it?"

"I'd love to."

Terry showed her through a retro 1960s kitchen. "Drew had it done just like my mother's kitchen was when I was growing up, except for all of the state-of-the art appliances."

Drew did all this for his mom? His thoughtfulness wasn't what most people would expect from a Wall Street fast-tracker, which Emily was certain he'd been. So how did he fit so comfortably into the mountains and Paradox when she, a native, never had?

Terry took Emily upstairs. "This is my room."

Once again the furniture was incongruent with the elegant design of the room. A nondescript bedroom set in some blond-colored wood, white sheer curtains and tan blinds.

"Oh, look at the carved molding. It's beautiful." One thing her mother had taught her was the knack of finding something good—no matter how small—in any situation. A skill that had come in handy during her Jinx years.

Terry opened the door to the right. "And this is Drew's room."

Drew lived with his mother? She peeked in. The room was decorated in a soccer theme, like a ten-year-old boy might choose.

"My grandson's been using the room when he stays over."

Relief flowed through her. She didn't want to think about what kind of grown-up man lived with his mother in a room decorated for a child. Thoughtfulness could only go so far.

"The room across the hall is the guest room. Drew put your bag in there. I'm afraid we haven't done much with it."

Terry opened the door. The room had nothing in it but a futon and her overnight case, which gave Emily a chance to admire the hardwood floors.

"I thought we should put carpeting in up here, in the bedrooms, at least."

"Oh, no. No carpeting. The floors up here are beautiful."

"That's what Drew said, too." Terry frowned and started back downstairs.

Emily followed. Obviously, Terry disagreed. But she let Drew overrule her. Interesting. Emily knew she shouldn't be thinking this. But how did Terry afford this home? She could see her owning it somewhere upstate where real estate was cheaper. But here in the metro area, it had to have cost a small fortune. It wasn't a home most civil servants could afford. Maybe it was a family home that Terry had inherited?

"Hey, Mom. I'm back."

Drew met them at the bottom of the stairs and smiled at her. Them. Why would she think he was smiling just at her?

"You're early," he said.

"My meeting was over before I got there."

Terry glanced from Drew to Emily. "You two go ahead and sit down and talk work. I want to put the roast in for dinner." She slipped off to the kitchen.

Drew motioned for Emily to go first. She took the chair his mother had sat in before and he sat across from her on the couch. "What happened?"

"The client wanted to go golfing this afternoon, so my boss rescheduled the meeting for this morning."

"And she didn't call you?"

Emily crossed and uncrossed her legs. "She gave me some excuse about knowing how much I probably wanted to get back down to the city and didn't want to take away my excuse for coming."

"Your boss took over your presentation?"

"I wish. She gave it, and the account, to one of my junior graphic artists."

"Bummer."

"To top it off, she ducked out on the lunch she'd offered. I could have stayed home and avoided the whole blow-up I had with Autumn about her having to stay at Jule's tonight."

"What? Then, who'd have my back at the birthday lunch with my mother, Scott and Jessie and their two rug rats?"

His tone was teasing but his expression held no trace of amusement. He seemed to be glad she was here with him. Her pent-up resentment about this morning melted away.

"Too true." She played along.

"Did Mom haul out the photo albums yet?"

"No, just showed me around."

"She must be saving those for later."

"It was fine. She made me tea and we talked. I didn't know you lived here when you were in New York."

"What?" His eyes widened in horror.

She hesitated. "Your room upstairs that you let your nephew redecorate."

Drew rubbed his chin.

"Your mother said he's been using it when he sleeps over."

He leaned forward. "That is *not* my room. I don't live with my mother."

She sunk back in the chair as far as she could as if buffeted by his words. "I feel like such an idiot. That was your room when you were a kid. Your mother made it sound like it still was."

He sighed and massaged his forehead between his eyes. "I haven't ever lived here. I grew up in an apartment a few blocks from here in a less gentrified neighborhood. I helped my mother buy this place just after the housing bubble burst a few years ago when prices were down. I put enough down so that she can afford the mortgage and taxes."

"That was really nice of you."

He flashed her a heart-stopping grin. "Not that nice if you consider everything my brother and I put her through growing up. I owed her at least that much."

"She doesn't believe that, does she?"

"No, so she acts like we both own the house with me owning the greater share."

"That's why she said you redid the kitchen for her and made it sound like you wouldn't let her put carpeting upstairs."

He shook his head. "She can put carpeting anywhere she pleases. All I did was point out what great shape the hardwood floors are in."

After a dinner at which Terry subtly played up Drew's strong points and he stared at his plate a lot, Emily offered to put the dishes in the dishwasher and clean up. Terry wouldn't hear of it. "You two go into the living room and set up the DVD player. I got the latest romantic comedy. Have you seen it?"

"Not me," Drew said.

"I did. I think you'll really like it," Emily said.

"If you say so." Drew drawled out the words.

"Not you. Your mother."

"He's always been incorrigible," Terry said. "I did my best."

"You know, she did," Drew said as they walked into the living room.

"So there's no hope?" Emily made herself comfortable on the couch, figuring Terry would want the chair.

Drew crouched down in front of his mother's DVD player to set up the movie. "What you see is what you get."

What she saw was a nice view of the contrast between the breadth of his shoulders, emphasized by the stretch of his polo shirt across them, and the narrowness of his hips. That aside, Emily wasn't sure of the validity of his state-

ment. Drew was—or had been—a Wall Streeter who did
well enough as a financial analyst to have made what had to
have been a significant down payment on this house for his
mother. He was also a mountain man, as her boss had called
him, and a handyman who was almost single-handedly re-
storing her family's lodge as part of getting ready to run a
summer camp for five hundred inner-city kids.

"There's some microwave popcorn in the cupboard, if you
want. I'm going upstairs to read." Terry picked up a novel
from the table next to the chair.

"You aren't going to watch the movie?" Emily asked.

"Oh no, I'd just be a third wheel. I'll watch it some other
time." Terry looked from her to Drew and smiled. "See you
in the morning."

Drew stood and crossed the room. The overstuffed cush-
ion dipped as he sat beside her. She reached for the remote
on the coffee as a cover to inch away from him.

The corners of his mouth quirked up.

Obviously, she wasn't as subtle as she'd wanted.

"Why does your mother think there's something going on
between us?" she asked.

A true smile spread across his face. "Mom? She thinks
I have something going on with any woman I mention. I
brought you home. And you fit the criteria."

She grinned. "You have criteria?"

The soft light of the lamp behind Emily framed her heart-
shaped face. Of course he had criteria, but that wasn't what
he was talking about.

"My mother has criteria. You're a professional with a job
that's likely to keep you in New York—once your term in
Paradox is over—so you'd want me back down here and
working on Wall Street once my summer of fun in the Adirondacks is over."

She pressed her lips together as if pondering that. "I didn't say anything that would make her think that."

"You didn't have to."

"Besides, it's not like you're vacationing in Paradox. You're working for the coalition."

"There's working and, then, there's working on Wall Street. My brother is the do-gooder. I'm the moneyman. Mom likes things to be a certain way. My being downsized threw off her equilibrium."

"And not yours?"

"Mine, too, but I got over it. And it doesn't help with Mom that Scott was married with Ethan on the way when he was my age. I've never gotten past being engaged."

"You're engaged?"

"Was. Was engaged," he ground out. If Emily was as smart as he thought she was she would drop this conversation thread right now.

Her cell phone chimed and the tension building in him ebbed. He turned the TV on to catch the sportscast on the news.

"She said what?"

He couldn't help overhearing her conversation despite trying to concentrate on the TV.

"No, I'm still here in New York. Yes. Thank you." She ended the call and tossed her phone on the table. "I can't believe it." She shook as she tuned to face him.

"Autumn." He muted the sound.

"That was Mrs. Hill. Jule called her mother and told her that I had come home early and asked if she could stay over at our house."

"Mrs. Hill didn't believe her for a minute."

"Not for a second. But Mrs. Hill thinks it was Jule's idea. They aren't crazy about Jule's boyfriend. She said they're walking that line between keeping a tight rein on Jule and not too tight a rein that they drive her to total rebellion and hoping the romance peters out when he goes away to college in the fall."

"Tough call." Would it have made a difference if his mother hadn't been working so much and had come down harder on him and his brother? Probably not. They'd needed the grounding in Christ Reverend Murdock had given them to straighten out.

"She also said she's sure Jack wouldn't have stayed. That he and Autumn aren't…"

Her cheeks turned crimson, and he wasn't sure whether he wanted to gather her in his arms to save her the embarrassment of facing him or tease it away.

He opted for teasing. "I told you Jack's a good kid."

She glared at him, her eyes bright.

"Which means Autumn isn't?"

"No, like you said, Jule cooked this up."

"But Autumn had to have gone along."

He couldn't win.

She rubbed the corner of her eye.

Think fast, Stacey.

"You don't know that. Could be that Jule was using Autumn as a front. Was planning to go somewhere else and let her mother think she was at your house."

"You think?"

He didn't know, but was leaning more toward Autumn being in on it.

Emily sniffled. He slid over and put his arm around her shoulders, like he would with one of his soccer guys who'd made a bad play. But that's where the similarity ended. Emily was a lot softer and smelled a lot better.

Emily looked up at him with a slight quiver in her lips. He bent toward her, drawn by her vulnerability, wanting to kiss the hurt away as he might with a child. But Emily was no child and that wasn't the kind of kiss he had in mind.

Chapter Eight

Emily stared at the ceiling and listened to the activity downstairs. It sounded like both Drew and his mother were up. She'd tossed and turned all night, and little of her restlessness had had to do with the thin mattress on the futon. Her thoughts had alternated between what to do with Autumn when she got back to Paradox and wondering if Drew had been about to kiss her last night or if she had imagined it. She didn't feel equipped to deal with either. They were going to service at Drew's brother's church. Maybe she could get some direction there. She forced herself to get up and get dressed.

"Good morning." Terry greeted her as she entered the kitchen. "What can I get you for breakfast? I'm making bacon and eggs for Drew." She nodded toward him standing at the counter near the coffeemaker. "He just got in from his run."

Emily took in his T-shirt and sweatpants. As if he needed the exercise. "Coffee is fine."

"You need more than coffee. It's no trouble."

"Toast. Jam, if you have some."

"Drew, pour Emily some coffee." Terry moved to the refrigerator and took out bread and jam. "Is whole wheat okay?"

"Fine."

Drew placed a mug of coffee in front of her without making eye contact and mumbled something about cream and sugar. He *had* been about to kiss her last night and apparently was feeling as unsettled about it as she was this morning. She picked up the creamer and stirred a dollop into her coffee. Across from her, Drew gave his full attention to eating the bacon and eggs on his plate. She almost laughed. Obviously, he hadn't wanted to kiss her any more than she had wanted his kiss. Or he wouldn't be so embarrassed this morning. She chalked it all up to his mother pushing them together all evening. Still, a part of her wondered what would have happened if she hadn't left when she did.

"Here you go." Terry placed a plate of toast and raspberry jam on the table in front of her. "I don't want to rush you, but we need to leave for church in about twenty minutes. If you're all set, I'm going to go get ready."

"I'm good."

Drew continued to concentrate on his breakfast until his mother was out of the room. "Listen, about last night..."

"Yes?"

He pushed the last of his egg around the plate with his fork. "You seemed like you needed a friend. I didn't mean to take advantage."

"Don't worry about it."

He flashed her a smile that had her glad she was sitting because it could have knocked her legs out from under her.

"I'm going to go get ready, too."

She pretended not to watch him leave.

Emily stumbled on the steps as the three of them left the house fifteen minutes later. Drew took her elbow. "It's these shoes." The strappy little sandals looked fabulous with almost anything, but could be a killer for walking. When she'd regained her balance, she started toward his parked truck.

Drew guided her in the opposite direction. "We usually walk to service."

"Scott's church is only a couple blocks away," Terry added.

A couple blocks could be at least one too long. Maybe she could jet back in and change her shoes.

Terry set off down the sidewalk. "The choir will be warming up in five minutes," she warned.

Emily toddled along to keep up with her and Drew. "Do you sing?"

"No, but my mother did when the boys were small," Terry said. "That's how I got them to church on time. If we got Mother to church late, the rest of the day could be very unpleasant. All I had to do was warn Drew and Scott that it was almost choir time."

"Gran lived with us," Drew said.

"It wasn't this church," Terry said. "It was in the old neighborhood." The last two words came out as if they carried an extremely bad taste.

"We started going here when Scott became assistant minister. That's when Mom moved to Cobble Hill."

"You'll like it," Terry said. "Our old church was so…"

"Mom." Drew's voice took on a low rumble.

"So working class. First United has class. A lot of members are young professionals."

Emily pushed her right foot forward in her shoe, so the back strap wasn't rubbing her heel. "It sounds a lot like my church in Manhattan."

Drew glanced from his mother to her and looked as if he was going to say something, but pressed his lips together instead.

Did Drew have a problem with a more reserved congregation? He did seem to fit right in with the big family free-for-all that was Community Church back in Paradox. She studied his stony expression out of the corner of her eye. A muscle moved in his jaw. There was more to this than his mother's offhand comment. More that she didn't need to know.

Emily was hobbling by the time they turned the corner to the front door of First United Church. From the people walking up the church steps, the congregation wasn't all young professionals, or even mostly young professionals. Two middle-aged women waylaid Terry when they walked through the door. She waved Emily and Drew on.

By the second hymn, the straps of Emily's sandals were burning a permanent indentation into her feet, or at least felt like they were. When the hymn ended and they sat, she unfastened the buckles and loosened the straps. The relief was immediate.

Before the scripture reading, a familiar-looking man stepped to the center of the sanctuary in front of the altar. "All children are invited to join me for the children's sermon." Another way Drew's church was like Community and unlike hers. At Emily's church, children had Sunday school and not many came with their parents to service. Or, maybe, their parents didn't come, either. The people she knew from attending services were mostly singles like her.

Children of all sizes trooped down the center aisle toward the smiling dark-haired man. A boy and girl sidled up next to him. There was something about his profile, his stance.

Terry whispered over Drew. "That's Scott."

Drew's brother. Of course, that's why he looked so familiar. They did look quite a bit alike. But Scott's features were less chiseled, and his physique not nearly as toned. Emily inched down the pew, suddenly aware of how close she and Drew were sitting. He turned his head toward her, and she buried her nose in the hymnal to find the next hymn, which she'd already marked with the bookmark ribbons. Emily did her best to ignore Drew's proximity and concentrate on the service.

After the closing hymn, Drew replaced his hymnal in the

holder on the back of the pew in front of them and waited for his mother to step into the aisle.

"Let's wait for Scott and Jessie and the kids," Terry said. She talked to people as they walked by. Soon Scott and his family made their way up to their pew. "I'll do introductions outside," Terry said over her shoulder as she joined her other son.

Drew let her into the aisle ahead of him. She took a couple of steps, and one of her shoes slipped off, pitching her toward the pew. Emily grabbed it and threw her other leg out behind her to keep her balance. She felt Drew close behind her and a sick feeling hit her as he tripped over her leg and fell sprawled on the floor. A boy behind him followed him down.

Heart in her throat, she glanced behind her. Some other parishioners halted the elderly couple behind them.

Someone lifted the boy up. "I'm fine," he said.

Emily shuddered and dropped to her knees beside Drew. "Are you okay?"

Drew grunted and muttered something that sounded very much like "Jinx strikes again." But he couldn't have. And she wasn't. Not here in New York.

"Can you move?" Her heart raced. He could have broken something. Or hit his head.

He pushed up with his arms and rose. "Nothing's broken. Just knocked the wind out of me." He frowned at the people circled around him. "Let's get out of the way. We're holding everyone up."

Emily took a lopsided step. "My shoe."

He raised his gaze to the ceiling.

"You go ahead. I'll meet you outside." She turned back to retrieve the sandal, not wanting to know if he'd gone ahead or waited. It was under a pew, the buckle trampled so it wouldn't fasten. She slipped the other shoe off and followed the end of the crowd out the door. Drew hadn't waited.

Emily listened to the pastor greet each person by name,

which was quite a feat considering how many people were there. "Good morning," he said when she reached him.

"Good morning, Reverend. I enjoyed your sermon." She had. Until her Jinx genes had kicked into action, she'd felt more at peace than she had in a long time. She couldn't remember the last time service had moved her so.

"Thank you. And it's Pastor John, please. John Hamill." He offered his hand.

"Emily Hazard." They shook.

"Are you new to the area?"

"I'm…I'm visiting. I came with Drew Stacey."

He looked out the door toward a small group that included Drew.

She rocked on the balls of her feet. "I had to go back for my shoe. It slipped off." She held up the broken sandal.

"So I heard." His eyes twinkled.

No! She would not, could not be Jinx here.

Drew watched Emily fly down the stairs to his right and his ex-fiancée approach them straight on in a perfect collision course. Emily veered to her left and arrived at their circle first. His mother began introductions. As she got to his sister-in-law, an all-too-familiar voice interrupted.

"Terry." His former fiancée, Tara, touched his mother's arm. She would choose today for one of her infrequent appearances at church.

"I'm glad I caught you," she said. "I'm not going to be able to make it for lunch today, after all."

His mother had invited Tara to her birthday lunch? He glanced at Scott who shook his head "no" imperceptibly. So, he and Jessie didn't know anything about it, either. One thing about Mom, she never gave up.

"I'm having an unexpected out-of-town guest." Tara turned toward Drew and Emily. She raised an eyebrow as if she'd just noticed Emily and gave her the once-over, spending extra seconds on her bare feet, before dismissing her.

Drew's temperature rose several degrees, and it wasn't a good rise.

"Mike Godfrey." Tara smirked. "You remember him."

Sure he remembered Mike. He remembered him giving an inordinate amount of attention to Tara when she was engaged to *him*. Drew couldn't say he was at all sad to see him go when Mike accepted a promotion in the Chicago office.

"Mike says the financial sector is picking up."

And, of course, Mike would know.

"There's a good chance we'll be hiring analysts in the fall."

Right when his camp gig was ending. He waited for his mother to pick up the ball and keep it in play. She didn't disappoint.

"Wouldn't that be perfect? You'll be back home by then."

Of course, it would be perfect for her. She wouldn't have to worry about her security. Not that she had to worry now. He'd reassured her of that again and again. But all of those years, squeaking by on her civil service salary and a prayer had formed her mindset. Helping her out was no strain. He'd been too busy working the past eight years, he hadn't had time to spend half of his enormous salary.

"And you will be, too, won't you?" Terry smiled at Emily.

"If everything goes as planned." Her eyes brightened as she smiled back.

Drew tensed. It wasn't enough that his mother and Tara were scheming ways to run his life. Now, Emily was joining in. He shook it off. Emily was simply stating her plans to return to New York when Autumn started college in August. They certainly didn't include him. He had his own career plans, or he would as soon as he solidified them. Plans that would let him stay at Paradox Lake. And he didn't need any help shaping them, not from Tara, his mother, Emily or his ever helpful big brother.

"I've got to run," Tara said. "Don't forget what I said about openings in the fall. You might want to give Rogers a call."

"Sure." His ex-boss held the bottom spot on his list of anyone he planned to call in the foreseeable future.

Tara slipped into a Mercedes convertible parked on the street.

"Time to get going," Scott said. "Our reservations are for twelve-thirty and they'll only hold them for ten minutes after."

His mother waved him off. "The restaurant is around the corner. We can be there in five minutes."

"But, ah." He eyed Emily's bare feet and the sandals in her hand.

"Not a problem. I'll slip them on at the door." She checked out the broken buckle. "I can make it to a table."

"And have a replay of the pile-up at church? Uh-uh."

Drew stepped between her and Scott.

"Back off, guys," Jessie said. "They can be such boys sometimes. What size shoe do you wear?"

"Seven."

"That's what I guessed. You all go ahead. We'll run back to the house and get Emily another pair of shoes." She waved the rest of the group off toward the restaurant. "Meet you there."

She motioned Emily in the opposite direction. "Our place is across the street."

Jessie led her into the apartment and to the master bedroom. She opened a walk-in closet to display shoes of every type and color. "I know. They're my weakness. I economize in other ways."

Emily laughed. "I really appreciate it."

"Take your pick."

She chose a pair of ballet flats. "No straps to break."

"Good choice."

She slipped them on and dropped the broken sandals in the wastebasket. "They're not worth repairing."

"Pity. They're really cute."

"Oh, well, I wouldn't get much use out of them this summer up north anyway."

"And by next summer, they'll be out of style anyway."

"I like your thinking."

They left the apartment and headed to the restaurant.

"I hope you weren't too put off by Tara. She doesn't have any hold on Drew anymore despite what she and my mother-in-law might think."

Emily picked up her pace. Not that it mattered to her if Tara did or didn't have a hold on him. "She's his ex-fiancée?"

"Yes. I can't believe Terry invited Tara to our family lunch, even if it is her birthday we're celebrating."

Emily cleared her throat. "I'm not family."

"But you're with Drew."

"I'm not *with* Drew. Not like that. We're just friends. We only met last week."

"And he brought you down for his mother's birthday? That says something."

"I had a meeting for work. It made sense to share a ride."

"If you say so." Jessie's eyes sparkled. "But have you seen the way he looks at you when you're not looking?" She laughed. "No, I guess not. He is definitely interested."

While she was flattered that Drew might be interested, she wasn't sure she wanted him to be. Not now when she needed to give most of her attention to Autumn and, if she'd read the undertones of yesterday's meeting correctly, hang onto her job. But if she *were* looking… Drew was someone she'd like to get to know better. Maybe in the fall when they were back working in the city.

Chapter Nine

On the drive back north, Drew responded to her comments and questions in polite monosyllables. She would have taken offense if she hadn't heard him and his mother talking downstairs when she'd been gathering her things from the bedroom. The words hadn't been clear, but the tone had been sharp. At West Point, about an hour out of the city, she gave up and closed her eyes to rest. But an urge to catch Drew looking at her when she wasn't looking and apprehension about confronting Autumn when they got home kept her from actually dozing off.

The truck crunched to a stop. Emily opened her eyes and righted herself before Drew finished saying, "We're here." He grabbed their stuff from the backseat and followed her in.

Autumn was in the kitchen, rather than holed up in her room as Emily had expected. An aroma of tomatoes and peppers emanated from the stove. She raised her guard. Unfortunately, what her short stint as a parent had taught her was to be wary of any unexpected signs of kindness or camaraderie.

"How was the concert?" Drew asked.

"Awesome. You should have been there."

Drew put Emily's bag by the doorway to the hall. "If you

ladies can manage without me, I'm going up to the lodge to check on the plumbing fix."

"Sure, go ahead." *Yeah, leave me in my time of need. You get to talk about the concert. I get to talk about after the concert.*

Drew ducked out the door.

"I've got stuff for tacos going."

"Sounds good. I'll go put my things away and come back to help you."

"You don't have to. I have everything under control."

Emily wished she could say as much. She carted her bag to her room and dropped it on the floor next to the bed. Autumn was up to something. Forgiveness for the stunt she and Jule had tried to pull on her and Mrs. Hill? That wouldn't come easy. Before Emily headed back to the kitchen for the unavoidable confrontation, she bowed her head and asked God for help in holding her temper and guidance in dealing with her niece.

Autumn was setting the table when Emily reentered the kitchen.

"It's all ready."

Emily sat and made her taco, mulling over how to start. She waited for Autumn to sit and finish putting her taco together. "Mrs. Hill called me last night."

"About Jule? I told her it wouldn't work."

Emily took a deep breath. "But if it had, would you have covered for her?"

Autumn placed her taco on her plate and looked directly at Emily. "Probably. We're best friends." She spoke the words matter-of-factly.

"Even though it would have been wrong?"

"Honestly, Aunt Jinx, don't tell me that you never…" She let the word hang as to let Emily fill in her own teenage indiscretion.

"Honestly." She repeated the word with the same emphasis

her niece had used. "I never had the chance with your Gram and Grandpa."

"I know what you mean. Remember, I lived with Gram and Grandpa until a few months ago."

Autumn was being so reasonable. Emily didn't want to be suspicious, but she couldn't help it. "You know there has to be a consequence for your actions. I trusted you."

"But I didn't do anything, not really. Mrs. Hill figured out what Jule and Ezra were up to, so I didn't have to cover for her."

"You were ready to help them do something you knew was wrong."

Autumn hung her head. It was a little much for Emily to swallow.

"I'm going to ground you for a week."

"Including the weekend? Jack and I have plans."

"You'll have to change them. I'm sure he'll understand. His mother said she didn't think he was in on Jule's plan."

Autumn made the same face she'd been making since she was a toddler when anyone stopped her from having her way. Emily stifled a laugh. "You have final exams coming up. Staying home will give you plenty of time to study for them."

Had she really said that? She sounded just like her mother.

A dark expression passed over Autumn's face. "I suppose I can live with it."

"You don't have a choice."

Autumn shrugged and dug into her taco.

Her niece's acquiescence caused the flutter of uneasiness in her stomach to do double-time. She picked at her dinner. If Drew were here… No, she wouldn't let herself be dependent on his gallantry, even though they'd agreed to team up. Autumn was her responsibility, and Emily handled her responsibilities herself.

Autumn got up from the table and put her dishes in the

dishwasher. "Tomorrow's trash day. I'll get the wastebaskets upstairs, if you want to get the kitchen container."

"Sure." Emily scraped what was left of her dinner into the container and tied off the trash bag. Autumn returned with the bag from upstairs and took it all outside.

As Emily put the new trash bag in, she saw a large envelope in the bottom of the container. It must have fallen between the old bag and the container. She reached in and pulled it out. The return address caught her eye. Autumn's other grandparents. She checked the postdate. Thursday. It must have come yesterday. News about Autumn's mother? Was that why Autumn was less prickly? Whatever was in the envelope was between Autumn and her grandmother. Emily tore the envelope into quarters and watched the pieces flutter to the bottom.

It was time to call in reinforcements. Tomorrow, she'd ask Drew to see if he could wheedle out of Autumn what her grandmother had sent her. For this evening, cleaning up the kitchen and checking her email was all she could handle.

Drew put the finishing touches on the last wall of the lodge's main room and placed the paintbrush across the top of the paint can. He looked around the room. Not too shabby. Not too shabby at all.

"Need any help?" Autumn asked.

"Hey. I didn't hear you come in."

"I didn't want to interrupt you." She crossed the room. "Looks nice."

"It does." He had to agree. "I'm done painting, but I could use some help with the cabin assignments. I've got a spreadsheet set up on my laptop."

She shrugged. "I was looking for something a little more physical. Lawn mowing, furniture moving. Anything. Four days of school all day and studying all evening is my limit.

I don't know why Jinx had to ground me for the weekend, too."

"Not my territory," Drew said. No way he was going to give any opinion on Emily's discipline. He folded the step-ladder he'd been using. "You can take this out to the shed and then I have new name signs to put on the cabins."

"Anything to escape the house."

"Uh, Emily knows you came down here?"

"Yeah, she released me to your recognizance."

He laughed. "It can't be that bad. You still have the phone, TV and computer."

"I've already had that lecture. I suppose your mother was like Gram and didn't let you watch TV or use your computer."

"We didn't have a computer. But worse than that, she didn't let me go to soccer practice."

"Harsh." She headed out the door with the ladder. "I'll be right back so you can tell me what to do with the signs."

This was the first chance he'd had to talk with Autumn alone, since Emily had asked him to find out what was going on with her and her grandmother. He'd thought about how to do it and had decided the direct approach was best. Either he'd find out or he'd have both of them ticked at him. Not a pleasant prospect. He went into the lodge kitchen and rinsed out the paintbrush, leaving it there to soak in soapy water.

"Cute," Autumn said when he returned to the main room. She dangled the new hiking trail tags that he'd strung on twine according to color. "Who knew you were so uptight." She nodded at the table. "All this and a computer-printed map color-coordinated to the tags."

"The word is organized, brat," he teased. "If you do a good job with the cabin signs, I'll let you help me retag the hiking trails tomorrow."

"Yes, please, anything to get out of the house. Then, I'll only have to get through Sunday. And Emily will have to let me go to Sunday school and church."

"She doesn't *have* to, but I think she will."

He ignored the dirty look Autumn gave him.

"The signs, hooks and hammer are on the porch. I'll walk you over and show you what I want you to do." Drew picked up the carved wooden signs, and she carried the hammer and plastic container of hooks.

He rubbed the back of his neck. Now was as good a time as any to ask. "So, did you hear anything else from your grandmother?"

Autumn stopped. Her eyes narrowed.

"Hey, I just asked. You don't have to answer."

She resumed walking toward the cabin. "Yes."

They walked the rest of the short distance in silence. He placed the signs on the bench in front and told her how to screw the hooks into the rough log siding and hang the signs.

"Go ahead."

She tapped a hook into the wood to get it started and screwed it in. He handed her the sign for that cabin so she could measure where to put the second hook. When she'd finished and hung the sign, she stepped back to survey her work. "The investigator found my mother." Her words came out in a rush. "He sent Nana her address and a couple of pictures. Nana wrote her. She thinks I should, too."

"Are you going to?"

"I did but I haven't mailed it. I don't have any stamps and, with the stupid grounding, I can't go to the post office to get any." She placed her hands on her hips. "I'm not asking Aunt Emily for one. She'll think I'm setting myself up to get hurt. I don't need her protecting me like I'm a little kid."

"If you're sure you want to do this, I have some stamps. And Emily is doing the best she can. She hasn't had all the practice your dad has."

"Neither have you, but you can stay cool about things."

"That's because I'm a disinterested bystander." He figured

the Lord might let him get away with a little stretching of the truth for greater good.

Autumn reached in her back pocket and pulled out an envelope. "Here's the letter. I was hoping you'd have a stamp or take it to the post office for me."

So much for his powers of persuasion. She'd planned on telling him anyway. He took the letter and put it in his shirt pocket. "Can you handle the other four cabins?"

"No problem." She gathered up the materials.

"All right. I'm going to go up to the house and then, to the hardware shore. I'll drop your letter off at the post office."

Autumn looked down and scuffed her toe against the porch floor. "You can tell her. About the letter. After it's sent. But make it clear I don't want to talk about it."

"I can do that."

Emily heard Drew's truck pull into the driveway and out again. He must have needed something from the garage, or maybe Autumn had driven him out of the lodge with her whining about being grounded. To listen to her, you'd think she'd been locked in a dark closet with no contact with anyone on the outside. The past couple of days, instead of holing up in her room as she'd done every day after school since Emily had arrived, Autumn had hung out in the dining room watching Emily work. Or not work. Autumn peering over her shoulder made Emily self-conscious. It wasn't that the teen wanted to talk. She was just there.

And when she wasn't, Emily's mind gifted her with replays of her and Drew in his mother's living room Saturday night. Emily willed her attention back to the computer. She'd better work while she had the chance.

A short while later, Drew's truck pulled in again. She turned off the computer and went to the kitchen to help Autumn with dinner. Drew was closing the refrigerator door. Her niece was nowhere in sight.

"I picked up some milk in town."

"You didn't take Autumn into town, did you? She's still grounded."

Drew ignored her accusatory tone. "Don't I know. I heard all about it."

"Sorry I snapped at you. She's been driving me crazy. Did she go upstairs?"

"No, she's finishing putting up the new cabin signs."

Emily held her tongue. It was hard to avoid asking him how he knew that's what she was really doing, since he'd taken off to town. Of course, she would have heard any car going by to the campground, and they were far enough out of town that none of Autumn's friends would have made the trek here on foot.

"I guess I'd better start dinner, then." She stepped around him and opened the bottom door of the refrigerator.

"Got anything in there I could barbecue? I picked up some propane while I was out, too."

"Aren't you handy?" She rummaged through the freezer until she found a package of chicken breasts. "I might just have to keep you around."

"Is that right?" he said, a lopsided grin on his face.

She looked over her shoulder before she stood. He was so close she could smell the scent of the woods on his clothes. The kitchen suddenly seemed so small. "I found some chicken." The package slipped out of her hand. She picked it up and shoved it at him.

"It grills better if you thaw it first."

"Of course." She grabbed the package back. Now if only her legs would work, she could stand and walk to the microwave.

"I'll go fire up the grill."

Thank You, God. She gathered her wits, what was left of them, and defrosted the chicken.

When it was done, she carried the chicken and a bottle of

her mother's homemade barbecue sauce out to Drew on the deck. "Here you go. Let me warn you that the sauce is spicy."

He took the meat and covered it liberally with sauce. "I can handle spicy if you can."

"Pour it on."

He raised an eyebrow. "Do you have a minute?" He motioned to the picnic table.

Her heart rate ticked up as she slid onto the bench.

"I found out what Autumn got from her grandmother last Saturday."

The ticking slowed. Autumn. Right. What else would he want to talk with her about?

He moved to the bench across from her. "The private investigator located her mother."

Emily leaned forward on her elbows. "For real? After all this time? Where?"

"San Antonio."

A lead weight of dread blocked her airways. "She's not thinking of doing anything crazy like running off to see her?"

Drew picked up her hands and held them in his. The blockage softened.

"No. Not that I know of. She wrote a letter. I mailed it while I was in town."

"You don't have any idea what she wrote?"

He shook his head. "Autumn volunteered the information about the P.I. and the letter on her own. I didn't push."

"I'm not supposed to know any of this?"

He squeezed her hands. "Autumn said I could tell you about the letter, but that she didn't want to talk about it."

She sighed. She ought to be thankful he'd gotten this much information.

The sliding glass door to the deck opened. "Aha! I caught you."

Emily jerked her hands from Drew's.

Autumn stepped onto the deck and shook her finger at Drew. "You send me out into the woods to do hard manual labor and here you are sitting sunning yourself on the deck."

"Guilty. Want to take over?"

"No, I think you're handling things fine." Autumn winked at him and headed back into the house.

Chapter Ten

"Jinx, over here."

Emily walked through the almost empty diner to a booth in the back where Becca Norton was waving to her. Brendon was asleep in his baby carrier on the floor.

"Not much of a crowd," she said as she slipped into the booth across from her high school nemesis or, more accurately, the wife of her high school nemesis.

"Breakfast is the big meal. I waitressed here my senior year, and the best tips I got were on days off school when I worked breakfast."

Emily tried to remember Becca working here, but she couldn't. Guess she'd done a better job of erasing the memories of her high school years in Paradox than she'd thought.

"Hope you don't mind sitting back here. There's more room here for Brendon's seat."

Emily's concerns on the way over that she wouldn't have anything to talk about with Becca may have been unnecessary. Maybe all she'd have to do is sit here and let Becca do all of the talking.

"So, how have you been?" Becca asked. She took two plastic-coated menus from the rack and handed one to Emily.

Emily scanned down the usual list of diner offerings wondering how rude it would be to say she'd been better. She went with a generic, "Good."

"I heard at the five-year class reunion that you were working at an ad agency in New York."

"Yep, I still am. Do you know if the Reuben special is good?"

"Matt orders them all of the time. I'm more of a club sandwich person."

Becca put her menu down. "I'm glad you could make lunch today. Much as I love being a mother, I'm going stir-crazy at home all day with no one but Brendon."

"Tell me about it. Telecommuting isn't as great as I'd imagined it would be," Emily said, surprised at how easy it was to talk with Becca. "And after eight hours of stir-crazy silence, I've been treated to a whiny teenager all evening."

"What's up with Autumn? She's usually pretty cheerful."

Emily eyed Becca to see if that was a dig. Old habits died hard. Nothing in Becca's expression gave any indication it was. "I had to ground her. And I made her study for her finals this week."

"That couldn't have hurt. When I went on leave, she was close to failing my Economics class."

"You're kidding? Autumn has always had great grades. Neal and Mom bragged about it to me all the time."

"Not this year. She wasn't doing too well in a couple other classes, either. Neal didn't tell you?"

"No." The list of things Neal didn't tell her was growing.

"I'm sure she must have brought her grades up, or you would have gotten a final warning letter from the high school."

"I haven't gotten any letter, so as far as I know, she must be okay on that count." Emily couldn't block the suspicions that filled her mind. Autumn always brought the mail in with her when she got home from school. She hadn't had any reason to think that her niece wouldn't share it all. Until now. Emily added a trip to the high school to her afternoon agenda.

She fiddled with her menu. "For not being busy, we're not getting very fast service."

Becca nodded toward the counter. "Some people are busy."

A waitress who looked familiar, but Emily couldn't place, was talking animatedly to three guys who seemed to be picking up lunch. Emily twisted around for a better look. One of the guys was Drew.

"Lori says those guys make her day."

Emily continued to watch Drew while her thoughts churned. She'd thought he packed a lunch to eat at the lodge. Or fixed something there. The kitchen was fully functional to serve up to one hundred people. It would be closer for Drew to have lunch at the house and make *her* day. Well, not *make* it. She had her work. But it would break up the day. He could bring his crew, too.

The rest of Becca's words sank in. "That's Lori Novak?" Lori had been their class valedictorian and on the cheerleading squad with Becca. She was so thin. Certainly not the voluptuous flirt she was in high school. But, apparently, still a flirt.

"I thought she went off to Stony Brook to study oceanography."

"She did. Finished in three years, and came back and married Stan Lyons."

All Emily could remember about Stan was that he skipped school a lot and drove a souped-up car.

"She has the sweetest twins. Girls. They're finishing kindergarten. It's so sad."

It was sad. Lori had such potential. And here she was working at the Hazardtown Diner. Just the thing she didn't want happening to Autumn.

"You know, right?"

"Know what?"

"Stan was killed a couple years ago, racing."

She'd had the hot car memory right.

"NASCAR. At Spencer Speedway out by Rochester. He was doing pretty well, driving for some outfit out there. Lori and the girls came back here and moved in with her parents."

"That's awful." Emily could have crawled under the table for the thoughts she'd had about Lori and Stan.

"There aren't a lot of year-round jobs here, and she finishes her shift before the girls get out of school in the afternoon," Becca said as if to address Emily's earlier less-than-charitable thoughts about Lori.

The guys left and Lori rushed over to their table. "Sorry." She flipped her pad open. "What can I get for you, Becca?"

Becca gave her order.

She turned to Emily. "Jinx! Without your braid, I didn't recognize you from behind."

"Lori. How are you? I usually go by Emily now."

Lori laughed. "Sorry. Everyone called you Jinx. I couldn't remember your real name. What can I get you?"

Emily ordered a Cobb salad.

Lori looked over her shoulder at the door the guys has exited. "Isn't he gorgeous?"

There was no question who she was referring to. And Emily had no argument there.

"I was telling him that my nephew's soccer team is losing its coach. The guy who's been coaching the team is moving. Drew coached a team in New York and really misses it."

As if she didn't already know that.

"I think he's going to do it. And you know who will be at all the games. To watch my nephew, of course." Lori tossed her oh-so blond hair and laughed.

"Is it a summer league? He's going to be pretty tied up with the camp," Emily said.

"No, fall."

"Oh, I don't know. We were down in New York last

weekend. I had a meeting for work, and it was his mother's birthday. He was talking with one of his former Wall Street colleagues and it sounded to me like he may be going back to his old job."

Lori's smile faded. "That's not the impression he gave me when I told him about the coach leaving." She flipped her pad shut. "I'll be back with your orders." Lori turned heel and walked to the counter to place their order.

"Was I too bad?" Emily asked.

"Yes, but I forgive you. She didn't know your real name. We only went to school together for thirteen years."

"I thought she was your close friend."

"We were on the cheerleading squad, but not good friends. She's not a particularly nice person."

"We're both bad."

Becca raised her hand like a stop sign. "I evoke Romans 8:33-34."

"Meaning?"

"'God does not condemn me because He has justified me. Jesus does not condemn me because He is seated at the right hand of God pleading for me in intercession.' I need all the help I can get."

"Becca, you're too much."

After lunch, Emily drove over to the high school in Schroon Lake, wondering why she and Becca hadn't hung out together more when they were in school. A sign on the main door directed all visitors to go to the main office. It was strange walking through that door as a visitor. A welcome blast of cool air hit her when she opened the office door. She'd forgotten that the only rooms with air conditioning were the main office, the guidance office and, maybe, the teacher's lounge. They'd always wondered about that. Of course, as usual, Mother Nature had favored final exams week with a mini heat wave.

"Can I help you?" a woman she didn't recognize asked her.

"I was wondering if I could talk with Ms. Ryder." She hoped she was still the counselor for eleventh and twelfth grade students.

"Do you have an appointment?"

"No, but it's important I talk with her."

"May I tell her what it's about?"

Emily tapped down her irritation. The woman was only doing her job. But she didn't want to discuss her personal business with someone she didn't know. She stopped short. Didn't that sound just like her mother? A smile curved her lips. "My niece, Autumn Hazard. I have temporary custody of her while my brother is serving in Afghanistan."

"Hi, you must be Neal's sister."

A friend of Neal's? A woman friend?

"Yes, I'm Emily Hazard. You and Neal are friends?"

"I'm Jamie Glasser. Neal and my husband are friends. My husband is deployed out of Fort Drum."

"Oh." She'd hoped Neal might finally be dating again.

"I know Schroon Lake isn't close to the base, but with John gone, I really wanted a job that matched the kids' school schedule, and Neal told me about the opening here. But you didn't come for my life's story. I'll check to see if Ms. Ryder is in her office." Jamie stepped to the phone and made a call. "She said to go right down."

"Thanks, nice to meet you." Emily started to leave.

"Wait, I almost forgot. You're supposed sign in." She pointed at a notebook on the counter. "I'm just filling in for Thelma Wood this afternoon. I'm actually the school nurse."

"So Mrs. Wood still runs the office?"

"With an iron hand, so I don't want to mess up."

Emily laughed as she signed her name, purpose for the visit and time of arrival.

"You'll need to sign out when you leave, too."

"Okay."

Entering the guidance office was like entering a second home. She'd spent a lot of time here talking with Ms. Ryder.

"Emily, hi." Ms. Ryder, an attractive, friendly woman about her brother Neal's age, met her in the reception area of the office. "I was expecting you." She motioned her to her office.

Expecting her? She'd only decided to come by an hour ago. Emily sat in the chair facing Ms. Ryder's desk. A wave of déjà vu hit her.

"You got my note?"

What note?

"No." Emily sighed, recalling Becca's mention of a warning letter. "I had lunch with Becca Norton and she said some things that made me think I should come in and see you." She rubbed the fabric of her slacks with her thumbs. "Is Autumn in danger of not graduating?"

"She was last week when I sent the note. Her grade in Economics was borderline, and she hadn't turned in her term project. Let me check with Mr. Havens to see where she stands in the class now. Autumn needs Economics to graduate." Ms. Ryder picked up the phone and had a short conversation with the long-term sub filling in for Becca.

"The good news is that she handed in her term paper and it was quite good. So she received a passing grade on it, despite the points taken off for handing it in late."

Emily's spirits lifted.

"The bad news is that she's still borderline. If she didn't pass the final exam she took this morning, she could fail and not qualify to graduate."

"How did this happen?" Emily asked herself as much as Ms. Ryder. "She's always been an honor student. And I know Neal doesn't let her run wild."

"Your mom and dad going down to Florida, Neal deploying, and a bad case of senioritis." Ms. Ryder shrugged. "I can't say for sure. She doesn't come in and talk with me like you did."

"Pester you is more like it. Looking back, I'm surprised you didn't gently tell my parents about the availability of professional counselors."

Ms. Ryder laughed. "It was my first year. I didn't know any better. But, seriously, I still listen when the kids need to talk, even if it isn't always on target with my job description. Autumn hasn't wanted to talk."

"Nothing I can do now, except pray she did well on her exam. She's okay in her other classes?"

Ms. Ryder typed some information into her computer. "Not great, but she's passing everything else." She clicked the mouse. "She's going to North Country Community, so her senior grades shouldn't affect her college plans."

And if she'd taken advantage of her early admission acceptance at Trinity, none of them would be going through this.

Ms. Ryder leaned back in her chair. "So how is Drew coming with the lodge renovations? Camp must be opening soon."

"You know Drew?"

"He's hired some kids to work for him through our part-time work program, and some of us have been trying to get him to join the singles prayer group at Community." A broad smile lit up her face.

Emily realized for the first time that Ms. Ryder wasn't merely attractive; she was beautiful, and probably no older, or not much older, than Drew. Her chest tightened with what had to be indigestion because she certainly was not jealous of her former guidance counselor. What did she have to be jealous about? Drew could belong to any group he wanted for any reason he wanted. It wasn't her business.

"I didn't know Community had a singles group."

"Yes. We meet on Wednesday nights. I never thought to invite you because you always talked about how your family was too tied up with church. You're more than welcome to join us." Her tone was sincere.

"I just might, and I'll ask Drew, too."

"Do that." Ms. Ryder smiled again.

Emily stood. "Uh, Lori Novak doesn't belong to the group by any chance?"

"Lori? No, why?"

"No reason. I ran into her today at the diner and she was on my mind." *And I was wondering if she was one of the "some of us" who wanted Drew to join the singles group.* She offered her hand. "Thanks for clueing me in on Autumn, Ms. Ryder."

The guidance counselor shook her hand. "Call me Erin, please."

"Of course. See you Wednesday."

Emily climbed into Neal's truck wondering what she was getting herself into saying she'd come to the singles group. She didn't join things, particularly church groups. Sunday service was enough for her. But she was looking forward to attending the group like she'd looked forward to lunch with Becca—whether or not Drew came with her. Although she certainly wouldn't mind if he did. She turned on the radio and sang along with Taylor Swift.

Drew pulled in the driveway just ahead of her. As she watched him hop out of his truck and lift his toolbox from the back with masculine grace and ease, she selfishly made a note to check out the singles group for herself before she repeated the group's invitation to him to join. After all, he probably wouldn't be interested if it was just a bunch of women.

"Hi," she called to him. "Done for the day?"

"For the most part. I left Autumn and the guys to clean up."

"Got a minute?" she asked before he turned to head toward the garage and the outside entry to his room.

"Sure." He opened the door for her. "What's up?"

Indecision silenced her for a moment. But he had said they should team up where Autumn was concerned. "Did Neal, or Autumn for that matter, say anything to you about her failing Economics?"

He leaned against the doorjamb. The scent of varnished pine filled the small space between them. He must have been finishing up the picnic tables today.

"No."

"Becca told me at lunch. So, I stopped by the high school and talked to her guidance counselor, Erin Ryder." She studied his face for a reaction to her mentioning Erin.

"I know Erin. She set me up with a couple guys to work part-time after school and on weekends."

His expression didn't give her a clue as to whether he had any interest in Erin beyond the employment program. Not that it mattered. Just because he had almost kissed her didn't mean they had anything going. But, for whatever reason, it bothered Emily that he might be interested in Erin, or any other woman. Jealous. She was jealous that a man she wasn't involved with might be interested in another woman. Or were they involved, or starting to be involved? Or was it that she wanted to be involved with Drew? She ment**ally** dismissed the questions. Any woman would be thrilled to have Drew's attention. But she couldn't have it both ways. And that really bothered her.

Emily dropped her gaze and toed a stone in the driveway to focus her mind back on their conversation. "From what Erin said, Autumn's grade was borderline at the end of classes. She sent me a letter I didn't get. The final Autumn took this morning will determine whether or not she passes. She can't graduate without Economics. What am I going to do with her?"

"You can't do anything about Economics and graduation."

She tensed. He was right, but he had to know that there was more to her question.

He moved closer and placed his arm loosely around her shoulders. "If she fails—and she hasn't yet—and Schroon Lake isn't offering Economics in summer school, maybe one of the other school districts in the county is."

He meant well, but that didn't particularly lift her spirits. "With all the state budget cuts, I don't know how many, if any, of the schools are offering summer school this year."

Drew squeezed her shoulder. The practical part of her knew she should pull away. She shouldn't pursue anything further than friendship with Drew until her responsibilities to Autumn were done. They'd have time for that in the fall when they both were back home in New York City. The rebellious, needy side of her leaned into him for comfort anyway.

"You know, it might not hurt Autumn to have to repeat Economics in the fall. Pay for her actions. She's the one who chose not to do the work to pass."

Emily shuddered and turned toward Drew. "You don't suppose she did it on purpose. To postpone moving into the apartment in Ticonderoga with Jule for community college?"

"Not on purpose. She doesn't think out things like you do."

Shades of Neal. Her brother often pointed out that Autumn wasn't Emily. Frustration gnawed at her. She was doing the best she could, using what had worked for her.

"Ask her."

Emily blinked Drew into focus. When had she moved so close to him?

"Ask Autumn about her grade and the letter, since she usually brings in the mail."

More confrontation. The frustration chewed through, turning her inside out. She looked up to glare at Drew.

"No one said it would be easy," he said.

She straightened. So much for his comfort. No, that wasn't fair. He and everyone else she knew in Paradox Lake were ready to help her.

Drew picked up the toolbox he'd left next to the door. "I'll catch you after I hit the shower."

She touched her fingers to her lips and watched him exit the door to the garage and the stairs to his room and bath. How arrogant. But she did feel more relaxed. Much more relaxed.

Drew peered through the window in the door before entering the kitchen. Emily was leaning against the counter next to the microwave smiling. Excellent. His bluntness hadn't sent her running. The afternoon sun shining through the window backlit her, bringing out the radiance of her skin and smile. He took an extra moment to enjoy her beauty before opening the door and stepping into the kitchen. "Hey, want me to talk to Autumn with you?"

The microwave dinged, and she took out a plate of spareribs. "All done."

He looked from her to the plate on the counter. The ribs or talking with Autumn?

"She called and asked me to defrost the ribs for dinner. So I asked her how her Economics exam went today. She said the exam was a breeze." Emily paused to take a deep breath. "Since she seemed to be in a good mood, I asked her about the note from Erin Ryder."

Emily's voice was much too cheerful for Autumn to have hidden the letter from her. It must have gotten lost in the mail, as unlikely as that seemed.

"She put it on my workstation, and I buried it." Emily pulled an envelope from her shorts pocket and waved it at him. "God was listening."

"He always is," Drew said automatically.

Emily handed him the plate of ribs and a bottle of barbecue sauce. "So, all I need you for is barbecuing these ribs. Autumn will be back to help with the rest of dinner any minute."

But he was beginning to think he might need her for more, a whole lot more. Drew took the ribs and sauce and made an exaggerated bow. "Your wish is my command."

A soft cool breeze rustled through the trees as he stepped onto the deck. He placed the ribs on the side of the grill and breathed in the mountain scent. A man could easily get used to living up here with its fresh clean air and magnificent views. His gaze ran over the high peaks in the distance to the kitchen window that framed Emily at the kitchen sink. If only he had a *real job* as his mother had drilled into him, something definitely lined up for the fall, rather than a half dream of running the camp year-round. Then, he could give into to his growing desire to know Emily "Jinx" Hazard better. A lot better.

Chapter Eleven

"Aunt Jinx, can you fasten this?" Autumn turned around and held up the clasp of the locket Emily's parents had sent their granddaughter as a graduation present.

"Sure." She took the two sides of the delicate gold chain. After avoiding a confrontation with Autumn over the letter from the guidance office, the week had gotten better and better. Autumn aced the Economics exam, removing any doubt about her graduating with her class, and Donna remembered to video conference Emily into the weekly production meeting this afternoon, where she was able to claim a prime job for herself. The only downside had been a subtle change in her and Drew's friendship. Not that she'd seen him enough since Monday to know whether the change was real or in her head. He'd spent so much time up at the lodge, it was almost like he was avoiding her.

She fastened the clasp. "Now, turn around."

Autumn spun and faced her, the skirt of her sundress flaring out and gently settling.

"You're beautiful."

Emily wished her mom and dad could be here to see Autumn as they'd planned. But Mom had called early yesterday morning to say they'd canceled their flight because Grandma was back in the hospital.

A whistle from behind her seconded Emily's observation. "And your aunt isn't too shabby, either." Drew walked over beside Autumn, his eyes glowing with an admiration that made Emily drop her gaze and fuss with the lay of her niece's locket. She centered it and recentered it in the V of Autumn's heart-shaped neckline.

Drew's sister-in-law's words about how Drew looked at her when she wasn't looking came back to her. She reached for the locket again.

"Aunt Jinx, I don't think you can get it any straighter."

"Oh, right." She dropped her hands and stepped back.

Autumn glanced from her to Drew, who had a bemused expression on his face. A grin spread across Autumn's face and she nodded wisely.

Emily wanted to set her thinking straight, except she couldn't know for sure what her niece was thinking. And she didn't want to set herself up for a Jinx moment where she denied that there was anything between her and Drew only to find out that wasn't what Autumn was smiling about.

A car pulled into the driveway.

"That'll be Jack and Jule." Autumn grabbed the bag with her white cap and gown and rushed out. "See you later." The screen door banged shut behind her.

"Alone at last," Drew said, rubbing his hands together sinister-style.

A shiver ran through Emily, even though she knew he was teasing. "Not for long. As soon as I get my purse and camera, we can join thirty other families in the high school gymnasium."

Outside, Drew helped her into the passenger side of the truck and walked around the front of the vehicle. The evening breeze tousled his still-damp hair causing a curl to fall across his forehead. He pushed it back. Drew was attractive in his usual T-shirt and jeans. Tonight, in a crisp sky blue dress shirt and pants, he was devastating.

"What?" he asked when he climbed in the driver's seat.

"Nothing," she said, rearranging her skirt on the seat.

He started the truck. "You were looking at me funny."

"All right." She lifted her purse off her lap and placed it on the seat between them. "I was thinking about how great you look."

He raised his eyebrows and a self-satisfied smile spread across his face. "Thank you."

That was it? No teasing? No something else?

"You're welcome."

They made the fifteen-minute trip to the high school in content silence and settled in with the other families on the gymnasium bleachers. A wave of sadness washed over Emily when the graduates began marching to take their seats in the chairs below.

Drew caught her gaze.

"I'm missing Neal. He should be here. And Mom and Dad, even though I understand why they couldn't come with Grandma back in the hospital." That she was Autumn's only family here weighed heavily on Emily.

"There she is," Drew said.

Emily moved forward to the edge of the bleacher to see better.

"Careful."

She looked over her shoulder at Drew.

"I don't want you to fall. Think of how embarrassed Autumn would be," he teased.

"I'm not going to fall." She leaned forward and the toe of her shoe slipped off the back of the footrest. Her stomach bottomed out like she was hitting the trough following the steepest rise on the Comet roller coaster at the Great Escape. She inched back on the seat, hoping Drew didn't notice.

Drew placed his hand over hers on the seat and left it there through the principal's welcome, the keynote speech by a three-time Winter Olympian alumnus and the valedictorian's speech on how important friendships are in high school.

Emily gazed over the crowd expecting to feel the disconnect she usually felt at local gatherings. When it didn't surface, she shifted in her seat. Drew glanced down at her and laced his fingers through hers.

The President of the Board of Education took the podium and began calling the graduates in alphabetical order. The air crackled with the tension of the people in the audience wanting to recognize their graduate's achievement but honoring the board president's request that applause be withheld until all the students had received their diplomas.

"Autumn Hazard." Emily's heart burst with pride, and a bit of relief, as Autumn walked up to get her diploma. She pulled her hand from Drew's and scrambled to get her camera focused. Neal would never forgive her if she didn't email him some pictures. She zoomed in on the board president presenting Autumn her diploma and clicked. Perfect.

"Did you get her?" Drew had risen and stood close beside her, his hand on her shoulder and attention focused on Autumn.

As she had with the previous student, the board president exchanged words, a hug and a smile with Autumn. Before she returned to her seat, Autumn searched the crowd until she found Emily and Drew. She raised her diploma in triumph.

Drew squeezed Emily's shoulder, and she slid her arm around his waist and hugged him back. Her face flushed at her public display. She sat down quickly and made a show of checking her shots on the camera, so she wouldn't have to meet the gaze of anyone around her.

He bent his head to hers. "Great shot."

She smiled. It was. Autumn looked so grown-up. What had happened to that chubby little toddler who had followed Aunt Jinx everywhere. Her eyes filled with tears.

Drew nudged her. "She just called Jule's name. Autumn wanted you to get her photo, too."

"Right." She snapped a shot of Jule and several other of Autumn's friends.

The last student returned to his seat and the board president motioned for graduates to stand. "I present the Class of 2011." In unison, the thirty graduates flipped the tassels on their mortarboards from right to left. The audience broke into loud applause. The graduates all filed out first, followed by family and friends. An arc of tables in front of the gym entrance offered chocolate chip cookies customized for each graduating senior and other refreshments.

Someone touched Emily on the shoulder. "I see she made it."

"Yes, she did." Emily hugged Becca, then pulled away self-consciously. What was with her and all of this hugging?

"I'm glad." Becca leaned closer to whisper in her ear, "I see you brought Mr. Gorgeous with you."

Emily started. Had Becca seen her hug Drew during the ceremony? And if she had, why should Emily give it a second thought. What was a little hug between friends? She glanced at Drew out of the corner of her eye. That's what they were. Friends. Right. They could work on the more-than-friends when things were back to normal in the fall.

Becca cleared her throat.

"Sorry, I was thinking."

Becca glanced at Drew and the corners of her lips twitched.

Emily couldn't do anything about the flush she felt color her face, but she could change the subject. "So how do you get to be here? Autumn said the tickets were limited. She gave her extra two to Jack and Jule, so all Jule's grandparents could come."

"I've been the class advisor since freshman year. So I get

to come and be a teacher, not a mommy, tonight. Matt's home babysitting."

Drew tapped Emily's shoulder. "I'm going to get some cookies and a drink. Want some?"

"No, go ahead. I'll catch up with you."

She turned back to Becca, who was watching Drew walk away.

"I hope you're working on that."

Emily remembered some of the reasons she and Becca had not been friends in high school. Becca had been so poised. She'd had lots of friends and never had any trouble attracting guys she wanted. Emily had pretended that she didn't care that no one at school asked her out. But she had.

"What?" Becca asked.

Emily tucked a nonexistent stray hair back into her chignon. As usual, her thoughts must have shown in her expression. She really did need to work on developing a poker face.

"I was just looking," Becca said. "I'm an old, happily married woman, whereas…" She nodded her head toward the refreshment tables where Lori was sidling up to Drew.

What was Lori doing here? Emily headed over to the table, where she overheard Lori saying, "My youngest brother graduated."

"Hi, Lori." Emily slipped her arm through Drew's.

He arched an eyebrow.

"What looks good?" She smiled at Lori.

"I don't know. I don't do carbs." Lori gave her a once-over that clearly said she found Emily lacking, then walked away.

Becca was right. Lori wasn't nice. But instead of the resentment she used to feel about being treated like that, Emily's first thought was that Lori was a very unhappy woman and she should pray for her.

"What was that about?" Drew asked.

"I guess Lori's on some kind of diet."

Drew pressed his lips together, but didn't say anything more.

"Look." Emily pointed. "There's Autumn's cookie with her name. I want to get a shot of it for Neal." She whipped out her camera.

"Careful," he said.

Emily's elbow just missed hitting Mrs. Donnelly in the face.

"It's okay. Take your picture," her former teacher said.

Emily did and put the camera back in her bag. "How are you?"

"Good, but a little sad. This may be my last graduation."

Was Mrs. Donnelly ill? She studied her face.

"Don't look so stricken. All I meant was that my last grandchild graduated today, Josh's youngest brother."

Relief streamed through Emily. "Have you heard from Josh?"

"My son's gotten several emails."

"Us, too. And Neal was able to call Autumn yesterday to congratulate her on her graduation."

"I'm sure she liked that."

"I just wish Neal could have been here, and my parents. Grandma's back in the hospital. I took as many pictures as I could."

Mrs. Donnelly squeezed her hand and filled some of the emptiness in her. "They'll have her college graduation."

If that ever happened. Emily knew she should be more optimistic. Lots of kids who started at community college went on.

"Now, mind your manners and introduce me to your friend."

The emphasis she put on the word friend almost made Emily laugh. She was pretty certain Mrs. Donnelly knew exactly who Drew was. When she looked at Drew, he, too, was fighting a smile.

"This is Drew Stacey. He's the manager of the church camp that will be starting week after next at the campground.

Mrs. Donnelly was my high school English teacher. Her grandson, Josh, is in Neal's reserve unit."

"Nice to meet you," Mrs. Donnelly said.

"You, too."

"So were you seeing each other in New York before you came up here to work on the camp? I saw you together at the party at the VFW for Neal and Josh and the others."

The Paradox grapevine at work. Not only did Mrs. Donnelly know who Drew was, but apparently she knew he was from New York and, if she was true to form, a whole lot more about him. She decided to let Drew field the question since Mrs. Donnelly had asked him.

"No," he said straight-faced. "We met when Emily came to stay with Autumn."

"You look happy together," the older woman proclaimed.

Emily waited for Drew to correct Mrs. Donnelly about their being together. Warmth infused her when he didn't.

"Oh," Mrs. Donnelly said. "My son is waving to me. We must be leaving. I'll see you at church on Sunday." She left with a wave.

"You didn't say anything," Emily said.

"About what?"

"Us. Being together." Was he being purposely obtuse?

"We are. You're here. I'm here." He paused and held her gaze with his. Her heart rate ticked up as she waited for him to elaborate.

"Aunt Jinx." Autumn's shout from behind her broke the thread holding them. Her niece rushed over with her friend Jule in tow. "Is it okay if I go right over with Jule and Jack to their house for the party? I know we were going to go get ice cream to celebrate first."

Emily worked to hide her disappointment. Getting soft serve was a little ritual of theirs. When her niece was small, Emily used to take her for ice cream whenever she babysat. Later, they'd celebrated milestones with a trip for soft serve—

Autumn's winning the sixth grade spelling bee, her making the regional finals in cross-country and her first date.

Emily cleared her throat. "Sure, but I want to get a couple of pictures of you with your friends first."

"Come on then, everyone's getting ready to leave." Autumn took off through the thinning crowd.

Emily turned to Drew. "Are you coming, or should I meet you back here?"

"I'll come." Drew placed his hand on the small of her back to guide her down the hall to Autumn and her friends. "And, afterward, you can take me out for soft serve, if you want."

She glanced up at him and crinkled her nose. His first impulse was to lean over and kiss the tip. Instead, he walked her down the hall to Autumn and her friends.

"Why don't you all get together by the wall?" Emily asked when they caught up with them. She snapped a couple of pictures like a pro.

"Now, the girls." A couple more clicks. "And one of you and Jule." The best friends slung their arms over each other's shoulder and hammed it up.

Drew spotted Jack on the fringe of the group. "How about one of Autumn and Jack?"

Emily shot him a look over her shoulder. One he was getting used to seeing, where she scrunched up her nose and pursed her lips. He wondered if she realized Autumn made the same face when things weren't going her way.

"Sure. Autumn and Jack." She hid her face behind the camera, motioned them in front of her and took a couple shots.

He wished she'd cut Jack some slack. Her attempts to keep Autumn and Jack apart could backfire and do the opposite. Maybe he should say something.

A remark by one of the teens made Emily toss her head back and laugh. A couple of curls escaped from the clip that held her hair up. *But not tonight. No need to spoil the evening by bringing up their differences where Jack was concerned.*

Autumn hugged Emily and waved to Drew before leaving with her friends.

"We might as well go, too," Emily said in a voice so soft he barely heard her.

"What? No more teachers to introduce me to?"

She shook her head.

He caught the bleakness in her eyes. *Better back off the teasing, Stacey.*

"Oh no, look. Autumn didn't take her cookie." Her voice quivered ever so slightly.

Without a word, he picked up the cookie and wrapped it in a napkin.

"Thanks." When she reached for the packet, her fingers brushed his and charged nerves that were already on alert.

"Shall we head to the soft serve stand?"

"I don't know." Her shoulders slumped. "That was mostly for Autumn."

He put his arm around her. "It's her night. She wants to be with her friends."

"I understand. I'm missing Neal. He should have been here."

"Yeah, but he couldn't be. You got some great pictures to send him."

"I did." Her eyes brightened a bit.

"I say we go to the soft serve stand, get ice cream and look at your shots."

"Ice cream again. You have a one track mind."

He pulled her closer to his side. She had that right, but it wasn't ice cream hijacking his thoughts. It was the willowy brunette on his arm.

Not good. Not now, his rational side cautioned. Not when he didn't have a real job, didn't even know where he'd be living in three months. A picture of the "soccer room" at his mother's house filled his mind. He blinked it away so that Emily filled his vision instead. Much better.

She smiled up at him and his heart rate quickened.

Or much worse.

The traffic in the parking lot was as thick as it ever got here, even during the height of tourist season. Thick enough to require all of Drew's attention, which gave Emily an opportunity to study his profile. The smooth slope of his forehead, patrician line of his nose, full lips, strong set of his chin. She'd admired it all before. But tonight something was different. Or, thinking back to the several times they'd touched and Mrs. Donnelly's questions, did she want something to be different?

Drew inched the truck to the head of the line and turned left onto the highway.

"Take the next right." She pointed ahead. "I know a back way."

"Leading me astray?"

The smooth timbre of his voice sent a ripple through her, "Is that possible?"

"I've been known to leave the straight and narrow."

"Take the next right." She concentrated on giving him directions to keep her mind from contemplating where such straying could lead.

He turned onto a heavily wooded road with no houses in sight. "Ah, the road less traveled."

The undercurrents of their banter got to her. She shifted sideways on the seat to face him. "Will you answer a question?"

"Shoot."

She breathed in and out slowly as if cleansing herself. "What's going on with us?"

His cheek dimpled. "That's easy. We're going out for ice cream."

Nice deflect. She fiddled with the leather strap of her bag on the seat between them. "As in a date?"

He hit the brakes hard and fast. "A squirrel."

Emily braced for another vehicle to rear-end them. Except they were the only vehicle on the road. She looked over her shoulder at each side of the road and didn't see any squirrel. *Shades of their first meeting.*

"Take a right at the next crossroads," she said as if she'd never asked that juvenile question. It must have been the stress of being back at the high school this evening.

"Yes."

Drew already knew the route?

"Yes, as in it's a date," he grit out. He cut the turn sharply.

Her stomach fluttered, and not from Drew's driving. He didn't have to sound so unhappy about it. It wasn't as if she'd pursued him or that she needed any more complications in her life, no matter how pleasant they may be, until she was back in New York in her real life.

"Right there." Emily pointed ahead to a small white building on the right side of the road.

He flicked on the directional. She had no idea how crazy she was driving him. He'd had no intention of making tonight or any night a date with Emily. But the way her face had crumpled when Autumn had said she didn't want to go for ice cream, he'd had to do something, even if it went against his better judgment. After the fiasco with his ex-fiancée Tara, he was going to lay off women for a while, at least until he knew what he was going to do careerwise—and where.

Drew pulled the truck into a parking space in front of the outside order window. Overhead, stars were appearing in the late evening sky with a vengeance as they could only in open country away from the city lights. Beside him, Emily sat motionless, seemingly as mesmerized as he was. However, if his radar was running true to form, the starlight display probably had her missing the city lights, counting the days until she'd see them again, while he was reveling in being here, far away from New York.

Abruptly, she jerked the door open. "Chocolate, vanilla or swirl?" she asked in a strained voice. "My idea, I'll treat."

"No, I'll get it." He bounded out of the truck and met her halfway in front of it. He'd said it was a date. He'd pay. A picture flashed in his mind of his mother at the kitchen table fretting about bills. He must have been about ten. A neighbor had paid him a couple of bucks for helping her carry groceries in. He'd pulled the bills from his pocket and put them on the table next to his mother. She'd smiled and said, "That's my boy," and kept the money.

"From the way you're frowning at me, I think it's in my best interest to let you. This time."

This was not going well. He took a deep breath and relaxed. "Maybe we should start over. Would it be better if I'd said this wasn't a date?"

"No, a date's okay."

She was okay with the date thing.

"But if we're having a do-over, you need to sound happier about it being a date."

He smiled. He could do that. It wasn't as if he were unhappy. Resistant. No, cautious was more like it.

"Better." She motioned him to the window. "I'll have a large swirl."

"I would have pegged you for a chocolate girl."

"You might have been right on the pizza, but you can't expect to read me correctly all of the time. I have my little surprises."

"I'm sure you do." He stepped up to the order window. "Two large swirls, please."

He handed Emily her cone and they sat at one of the picnic tables. He watched her savor her treat, carefully licking around the edge of the sugar cone.

"What?" She caught him staring at her and momentarily halted her attack.

"Just enjoying the evening and you."

The smile she flashed him surpassed the one he'd gotten when he'd handed her the soft serve.

So she liked him looking at her.

"You might want to pay attention to your ice cream, too."

A cold, sticky drop rolled over his knuckles. He lapped it up and cleaned up the rest of his cone, prompting a giggle from Emily. *A giggle.*

He loved it. If only everything could be as simple as this moment.

The next day, Emily hummed to herself as she folded laundry in the basement. The remainder of her and Drew's evening had chased away some of her doubts about their relationship. After all, they'd soon both be back in the city and could continue seeing each other and see where things went.

Autumn clomped down the basement stairs. "What's up with Drew?" she demanded.

"Good morning, or I should say afternoon, to you, too." Emily wasn't sure what time Autumn had gotten home, except that it had been late—or early, early this morning.

"Did you say something, do something? He's moving all of his stuff out. I saw him out the window loading his truck."

"No." She hadn't, had she? Emily stopped folding the towel in her hands and played back their evening in her mind. She hadn't done anything Jinx-like at all. But that knowledge didn't slow her hammering heart.

"We could go ask him." Emily refolded the towel and tossed it in the clothes basket.

"Will you? I was afraid to."

Autumn looked so young in her jeans shorts and Winnie the Pooh T-shirt hopping from one bare foot to the other and winding a strand of hair around her finger. "I mean, Daddy wanted him to stay with us. Remember, he said that before he left."

It struck Emily like a steamroller. Autumn must be feeling all alone like she so often did as a teenager. But not because Autumn felt like she didn't have any friends and didn't fit in here in Paradox. Rather, it was because she did fit in and everyone else had left or was leaving—Emily's parents to take care of Grandma in Florida, Neal for Afghanistan, Autumn's friends who were going away to college and Drew. Although Emily suspected his move was only up to the lodge. And in a short time, Emily would be gone, too. She shared a pang of Autumn's loss.

"Sure. I will. He's probably taking some of his things to the lodge. Camp's starting soon."

"But why all of a sudden without saying anything, and it looks like a lot more than some."

"Come on." Emily headed up the stairs with Autumn trailing behind, much like she did when Emily was a teen and Autumn dogged her every step whenever she could.

As Autumn had said, Drew was loading what looked like all of his belongings into his truck. Emily paused to look at him as he lifted a large box.

"Hi, what's going on?"

Drew turned and smiled at them. "Packing up my stuff to move it to the lodge."

Emily shot Autumn an "I told you so" look.

"But…" Autumn stepped up next to the truck. "Camp doesn't start until the first week of July, and you didn't say anything about moving out."

Drew glanced from Autumn to Emily. "Do you want to tell her?"

Tell her what? Emily searched her mind for a clue as to what Drew was referring to.

He rubbed the back of his neck and shifted from foot to foot, "Uh, Emily and I are…"

She stopped breathing. *Are what?*

"We're...sort of...seeing each other."

Emily would have laughed if he hadn't made it sound like something akin to a fatal disease.

Autumn squealed. "I knew it." She pointed at each of them. "This is great!"

Emily marveled at her niece's complete about-face in emotions.

"But what does that have to do with you moving down to the lodge?"

"You know..." He shrugged. "It looks better. Seems right."

Autumn rolled her eyes, so Emily didn't have to. He could be too adorable at times. She'd better give him a hand.

"He's right. It's a small town. People talk."

Autumn faced them, hands on hips, a big grin splitting her face. "You know what would be really cool?"

Emily almost hated to think.

"It would be really cool if you both stayed here, like permanently."

A smile almost as wide spread across Drew's face, and it hit her full force. Drew would really like to stay here. But she had to go back to New York. That's where her job was, her life, all that she'd dreamed of and worked so hard for. She couldn't give that up. She just couldn't.

Chapter Twelve

"Aunt Jinx!" Autumn shouted from the kitchen door. "Aren't you coming down to help? We've been working all morning. Everyone is down at the lake."

"Not you," Emily called back.

Autumn appeared in the dining room doorway. "Funny! Drew sent me to town to get gas for the chain saws. What a mess. The winds last night did a real job."

The storm had been spectacular and ferocious.

"Branches are down all over, and the roof of one of the cabins is half caved in. The campers start arriving tomorrow. We need all the help we can get."

But maybe not her help. Emily turned from the computer. "Give me a half hour. I need to finish this first."

"If it makes any difference, Drew said to pick you up on my way back."

Emily smiled. "I still have to finish." *And prepare myself.* Emily had lots of experience getting the campground ready for the summer, most of it bad. She'd been the only one in her family to have a run-in with poison ivy, more than once, upset a hornets' nest, and trip over a stump and break her arm, not to mention all of the sunburns. And those were the summers she remembered. Who knows what outdoor mishaps she may have had when she was small that she couldn't remember. Eventually, her parents gave her the tasks of getting the insides of the larger house cabins ready and coordinating the camping registrations.

"But I'll tell Drew you'll be down."

"Yes, I'll be down."

True to her word, a half hour later Emily drove down the gravel road to the waterfront. Autumn hadn't exaggerated about the wind damage. Fallen limbs were everywhere. They were lucky they hadn't lost power.

Drew waved to her as she drove by him and pulled into the parking area next to the lodge. She hopped out of the truck and walked over to the lodge porch. Becca Norton sat in an Adirondack chair with Brendon on her lap reading a story to two little blond girls and another little boy seated on the floor.

She smiled at her and kept reading. Emily waited for Becca to finish. She could do this. Watch the kids, if Becca wanted a break to go help the others with the grounds cleanup.

A minute later, Becca closed the book. "Hi."

"Hi, up for a replacement?"

Becca looked past Emily toward the beach where a group of people were filling a trash bag with debris. "I wouldn't mind getting out in the sun for a while. Can you believe how beautiful today turned out, after last night?"

Emily shaded her eyes and gazed at the lake, drawn by the sunlight dancing on the water. The view got even better when Drew strode into it. He hiked up the path to the lodge, trailed by a dark-haired boy who looked to be about nine or ten.

"Drew," the two little girls cried and pushed by Emily. They wrapped themselves around his legs. The dark-haired boy shot them a look of disgust.

"So, who are your friends?" Emily asked.

"Jamie Glasser's kids. She's the camp nurse."

"Right. I met her at the high school."

"Yep, that's her. These squirts are Rose and Opal." He disengaged the girls. "And this is their brother, Myles. He's helping me out today."

Myles looked up at Drew with admiration in his eyes.

"The little guy with Becca belongs to one of the church members I don't know."

Becca filled in the name of one of their high school classmates. Emily was surprised at how many of them had kids. No one she knew in the city did.

"You're just in time to give us a hand," Drew said. "We're going to repair the roof on one of the cabins."

He couldn't expect her, Jinx Hazard, to climb up on a roof. She scanned the grounds. Like Autumn had said. Everyone was here. The locals really pulled together when there was a need.

"Oh, I told Becca that I would relieve her here."

"You don't mind, do you?" he asked Becca.

"Not at all." She gave Emily a knowing smile.

"Let me put on some sunscreen." She lathered the lotion on her arms and face and the back of her neck. "Ready."

"We already carried the ladder and shingles over. The guys who helped me with the work on the lodge did most of the repairs. We need to get the shake shingles on."

Emily hid her amusement when Myles solemnly nodded in agreement.

They walked along the lake path, people in the work crews waving as they passed by, and into the woods. Drew stopped at the third group cabin they came to and he pointed at a downed branch the size of a small tree.

"That's what hit it. We're lucky there wasn't more damage. Let's get to work. You can hold the ladder."

Relief flowed through her. She could do that.

Drew propped the aluminum extension ladder against the side of the cabin and tested it for stability. The bright new wood used to repair the damage sharply contrasted with the weathered old shingles that covered the rest of the roof. He picked up a hammer and box of nails from the toolbox next to the cabin.

"Once I'm up the ladder, hand me the nails and the shingles as I need them."

"Okay," Emily and Myles said in unison.

Drew started up the ladder. Once he'd gotten up a couple of rungs, Emily grasped either side and leaned her weight into it keeping it steady. Drew climbed two more rungs, and the ladder jerked to the right.

"Get back," Drew shouted as the ladder began to slide.

Emily's heart pounded so hard she couldn't breathe. The ladder ripped from her grasp.

"Cool!" Myles said as Drew jumped free before the ladder took him down with it.

"I...I couldn't...hold on to it."

Drew stared at her. Emily thought it was her fault? Did she think anything bad that happened when she was in Paradox was somehow caused by her? Although Drew was sure they meant no harm, the Jinx nickname her family and others had stuck on Emily had really done a number on her.

"I'm sorry."

A rush of anger raged through him. "No need." His voice was gruffer than he meant it to be. "I should have checked the ground for soft spots. The right leg sunk in the mud."

He motioned her over to see. "I must outweigh you by fifty pounds. No way you could have held the ladder once it started sliding."

"I tried."

"That you did. Magnificently." This self-effacing facet of Emily was new and brought out the protector in him. Not that Emily usually needed protecting. But he liked the feeling.

"Come on." He motioned to Myles. "I need help moving

one of the flat shale rocks from the cabin steps over here to put under the ladder."

Emily's subdued grin said she knew he didn't need any help. And he liked that, too. If only she were more open to sticking around Paradox Lake. They could have real possibilities. That is, if he had a definite, steady job that would allow him to stay here.

The rest of the roof repair went off without a hitch, and by seven o'clock when most of the volunteers had left, the campground was looking ready for tomorrow's invasion of campers. Autumn and Jack and a couple of other kids from the youth group had started a fire in the fire circle on the beach. Emily was sitting by herself on the dock.

"Hey, want me to cook you up a hot dog?" Autumn waived a stick toward the fire as Drew walked by. "We all chipped in, and sent Jack to the grocery store in Schroon Lake to get food."

"Sure. I'll see if Emily wants one, too."

"I'll give you a shout when they're done."

"Thanks."

He continued to the dock, stopping a few feet away to study Emily's delicate profile silhouetted by the blue water. The fading sunlight brought out the rich honey color of her long braid and the wisps of hair that had escaped it.

She looked back at him. "It's beautiful, isn't it?"

He couldn't disagree with that. Both she and the view of the lake backed by the mountains were beautiful.

"I'd forgotten or had just taken it for granted until I moved away."

He lowered himself to the dock next to her.

She cocked her head to the side. "You said you and Scott went to camp up here. Where?"

"Camp Sonrise on Schroon Lake. I loved it. It's closed now."

She nodded.

"I hated to go home when our two weeks were up. I used to wish I could stay here forever. Still do. But I need to find decent work."

"Fat chance, if you're looking for anything like you had on Wall Street." She drew her knees up and wrapped her arms around them.

"I might be able to get a back office position with a bank or mutual fund company that I could do long-distance." Not that he was all that keen on getting back into finance. But it was what he did. "You're doing okay with your telecommuting."

She pulled a face.

"Come and get it," Autumn shouted.

Drew stood and offered Emily his hand. It felt so soft and small in his. "Not so good?" he asked.

She shrugged. "It's okay, I guess, on a very temporary basis, like your job here at the lake. But I couldn't imagine doing it long-term."

Some of the magnificence faded. The problem was he *could* see staying here long term.

Emily set up her laptop in the main room of the lodge for the PowerPoint presentation she'd put together for Drew's middle-school-age campers. She'd been uncertain when Drew had come to her yesterday with his problem. The young art teacher/counselor who was running the camp art program had a death in the family and had to go out of town today, the first full day of this camp session. The other counselors could fill in for him for the one day, except for a special week-long program some of the middle school students had signed up for. Drew didn't want to shortchange them—or their parents.

"Ready?" Drew asked as he entered the lodge.

"I guess. You think the kids will be interested in what I do at work?"

"As interested as they'll be in the other sessions on art jobs scheduled for the rest of the week."

He leaned his hip against the table. "I really appreciate your doing this. So far, the first few weeks of camp have gone off without a hitch."

"Except for the late plague of black flies."

"That sort of thing is to be expected. And believe me, a disgruntled group of middle schoolers is far more threatening than a swarm of bloodsucking insects."

"Just the information I need to bolster my disappearing confidence in this presentation."

"You'll be fine. Got any candy?"

Why hadn't she thought of that?

"I'm kidding."

She laughed off some of her tension. "From what I remember of Autumn at that age, candy would have been a good idea."

"I almost forgot. Add Jamie's son Myles to the group list. He's only going into fifth grade, but is really interested in art."

Drew sure was taking an interest in Myles. She'd heard all about his skills in soccer, along with numerous other anecdotes about the boy. Or maybe Drew had an interest in Jamie. No, now she was being silly. Jamie was married, happily so from a conversation they'd had the other day. Besides, it wasn't like Emily had dibs on Drew. Did she? Still, a twinge of jealousy remained.

The camp bell rang, and the kids bounded out of the lodge on to their next activity, which was free time. The presentation had gone better than she'd expected. She hummed to herself as she packed up her computer.

"Good job."

She dropped the power cord she was winding. "You were watching me?"

"Yeah, I had a great view from my office." His eyes sparkled.

Emily ducked her head and concentrated on rewinding the cord so he wouldn't see the blush warming her cheeks.

"Have you ever thought about teaching?"

"Me? No, not in a million years. I'm much more of a business person. I like the pace of advertising."

"You were really good with the campers."

"Yeah, as a one-time thing. I can't imagine doing it every day."

"Becca and Jamie like their jobs at the high school."

What was he getting at? Did he think she should quit her job in New York, move back here and teach?

"No comment?" The spark in his eyes dimmed. "Don't days like this make you want to figure out some way to stay here?"

Ah, he'd succumbed to the lake's summer allure. It *was* appealing. But, by the end of the summer, she was sure he'd be as ready to go back to New York as she was.

"Nope." Staying in Paradox Lake wasn't a conversation she wanted to get into. She'd had it often enough with her parents and Neal.

He smiled a crooked smile. "I tried. Do you have to go right back to the house?"

"Not really. What do you have in mind?"

"There's going to be a pickup soccer game. Counselors and kids."

Emily warmed to the invitation to spend time with Drew. But she had always avoided organized sports like the plague. "I'm not much of an athlete. How about a walk along the beach?" She watched his eyes intently to see if she'd been too forward. He did seem to want to spend time with her.

"That would be great."

Her pulse quickened.

"But I promised Myles I'd be on his team. He's kind of latched on to me. Jamie said he misses his dad."

Jealousy stabbed her again. But it wasn't Jamie. That had been a crazy idea. Nor was it Lori or any of the other eligible local women who seemed to be putting themselves in Drew's path. No, it was the way he was slipping into small town life. A life she'd willingly given up.

She was jealous of Paradox.

And she wasn't sure what to do about it.

Chapter Thirteen

"Achoo!" Emily sneezed as she swept out months of dust from one of the two rental house cabins. She looked through the trees to the lake. Who would have thought? Not only was she getting the cabins ready for the two families who were renting them for the last two weeks of August, but she was enjoying herself. Looking forward to seeing the long-time renters, who'd been coming to Lakeside for almost as long as she remembered.

Getting back to work, she shook her head in tandem with the sweep of the broom. What had happened to the vow she'd made to not have anything to do with her family's business when she moved out at eighteen? If she didn't watch herself, she'd be taking her parents up on their offer to give her a share of the campground. She sang along with her iPod as she put the broom aside and tackled cleaning out the wood-stove. The nights might get cold enough to use it.

"So, do you do windows, too?"

Emily dropped the grate which hit the lip of the opening with a clang.

"You startled me," she said as she rose and turned to face Drew. "And, no, I don't do windows."

"I was afraid of that." He walked across the room and

squatted down in front of the stove. He poked his head in the stove's open double doors.

"You should see if you can get a chimney sweep out before your vacationers arrive."

"I can do that."

He stood and wiped his hands on his jeans.

"So, what's up?" she asked. "Did the hordes of happy campers drive you from your office or are you moonlighting as a vacation cabin inspector?"

He stood and turned to face her.

"Not that I mind. With you and Autumn working at the camp all day, I get a little lonely for verbal contact sometimes. I can only talk to myself so much."

"Lonely cleaning staff." He pretended to check off an item on an imaginary clipboard. "I might have a solution for that." He brushed a stray strand of hair behind her ear.

Emily's heart raced. He was going to kiss her.

The cabin door slammed open and closed, and he jerked back.

Autumn rushed in. "I've been looking all over for you. Have you heard from Daddy?"

Emily blinked to bring herself back to reality and her niece into view.

"Have you?" Autumn demanded, gesturing wildly and bouncing on the balls of her feet.

"Not when I checked my email this morning. I've been working here for the past few hours. What's wrong?"

"Jule called me. She was down at the gas station, and she heard that Josh Donnelly got hurt, bad." She gulped for air. "The unit got ambushed. And I haven't heard from Dad in days." The teen burst into tears.

Heart pounding, Emily gathered Autumn into her arms and smoothed her hair.

"I can't go back to the house." Autumn hiccupped. "I'm afraid officers will be there."

Emily's chest constricted. "Honey bear." She used the family's baby name for Autumn. "Your dad might be trying to contact you right now to let you know he's okay. I'll go back to the house with you. I can finish up here tomorrow."

"I'll call Pastor Joel," Drew offered. "I'm sure Josh's family will have added him to the prayer chain if he's been hurt."

Emily's heart swelled with appreciation.

"Could be Jule heard wrong or the person she got her information from didn't get the facts straight," Drew said.

Autumn tore into him. "Yeah, like they aren't hurt, they're dead." She streaked out of the cabin.

Drew's face went slack. "I was trying to be positive."

She patted his arm. "I know. I'd better run and catch up with her. Let me know what you hear."

"Are you okay?"

"As okay as I can be." She dashed off after her niece.

Autumn was almost back to the house by the time Emily caught up with her. Once she got Autumn in the house, sat down and settled with some tea, she checked her email on her iPhone. Nothing from Neal. Autumn's gaze didn't leave her as she hit the off button and picked up the house phone. She punched in the voice mail number.

"You have one new message." Her heart raced. "Press one for new messages." She pressed one, and Autumn's eyes widened.

"Hi, it's me," her mother's voice said. "Checking in. Your grandmother's doing much better. Call back when you can."

Emily hung up. "That was your gram."

Autumn put her tea mug down, hard. "Did she hear something? Is that why she called?"

Emily shook her head. "No. All she said was that Great Grandma was better."

"I'm going to call her." She whipped out her cell phone before Emily could suggest she wait until Drew got back.

"Gram?" Autumn's voice had a screech quality to it. "Have you heard from Daddy?"

In the moment of silence that followed, Emily slid into the chair next to Autumn.

"You haven't, either? Josh Donnelly's been hurt in some kind of ambush, and Daddy hasn't emailed or called for days. I'm so scared that something's happened to him, too." Her words tumbled out one on top of another. "I can't calm down." Autumn's face contorted. "How am I supposed to calm down?" Tears streamed down her cheeks. "And nobody else cares. Aunt Jinx was too busy with Drew to even listen when I told her."

Her stomach churned. That's what Autumn thought? That she didn't care? Her mother didn't need this. She didn't need this. Emily reached over and gently took the phone from the teen's hand. Autumn stared at her defiantly.

"Mom, are you still there? It's me."

She kept her gaze on her niece. Autumn pushed away from the table with enough force to knock over her mug and rushed from the room. Emily watched the narrow rivulet of tea dribble from the tipped mug and inch across the table.

"Yes, she's really upset. She's run off to her room. Yeah, I'll let her settle down a little. No, I don't really know what's going on." She told her mother what Autumn had heard and that Drew was checking with Pastor Joel.

"I'm sorry to hear about Josh Donnelly. But I'm sure Neal is fine. Autumn can be a bit of a drama queen." Her mother reassured her as she'd tried to reassure Autumn.

"I just hope one of us hears something from him soon."

Her father said something in the background.

"Yes, I'll tell her." Her mother said back to him. "We got a letter from the coalition of churches asking if we'd be interested in leasing them the campground year-round. Nothing definite, but your father is already making plans. Improvements he could make. He's anxious to get home now that your grandmother is doing so much better."

Mom was trying to keep the conversation light, but worry edged her voice.

"I'm not surprised. For Dad no place comes close to Paradox Lake." And Emily suspected Drew felt almost as strongly. But, unlike her dad, Drew's career opportunities were in New York.

"And speaking of the coalition and the campground, what did Autumn mean, you and Drew?"

Emily sensed that her mother was keeping the conversation going so she wouldn't have to hang up and tell her father about Neal.

"Like you and Dad said, he's a good guy."

"You've been seeing each other?"

"We're friends."

"Just friends?"

"Good friends, for now. I still have Autumn to look after. We'll see what happens when Drew and I are back in New York in the fall."

"Oh honey, if you have feelings for him, don't push them off. Something could happen."

Her mother's voice caught, bringing Emily's thoughts back to her brother.

"Mom, are you okay?"

"Yes, but I'd better hang up and tell your father about Neal. Love you."

"I'll let you know as soon as I hear anything. Love you, too."

Emily turned the phone off and leaned on the table for support. The tea continued its progress across the table. When it reached her hand, she shook off the liquid and went to the sink to get the dishcloth to wipe it up. She was still rubbing at the table when Drew let himself in a few minutes later.

"What did you find out?" she asked.

Drew put his arm around her shoulder and pulled her close to his side. Her heart sunk.

"Josh Donnelly was hurt. Bad. He's being transported to a base hospital in Germany."

"Oh, no," she said softly. "Neal and the other guys?"

"I don't know. Joel only knew about Josh. Where's Autumn?" Drew asked as if he'd just noticed she wasn't there.

"Up in her room. She called Mom and had a total meltdown. I figured I'd give her some time alone."

"I'm not sure that's good," he said.

She slipped out from under Drew's arm. When did Drew become an expert on teenage girls?

"We should check on her. I'll tell her what I found out."

Emily hesitated. If it had been her, she'd want to be left alone. In fact, she wouldn't mind being alone now. She could go to sleep and maybe everything would be better in the morning. Of course, as her brother had told her ad nauseam, Autumn wasn't her. And as drained as she felt, it was too early to go to bed.

"All right." She relented. "But let's play down the hurt bad part."

They trudged upstairs. Emily's knock on the door garnered an inaudible response. She opened the door to find Autumn facedown on the pillow, her laptop running beside her.

"Can we come in? Drew's back. He talked with Pastor Joel."

Autumn rolled over on her back not looking at them. Emily walked over and sat on the edge of the bed next to her. She smoothed her hair back out of her eyes. The teen pushed her hand away.

"What did Pastor say? I was right, wasn't I?"

Drew stood at the end of the bed gripping the wooden footboard. "Josh was hurt. He's in a base hospital in Germany. His dad called Pastor early this morning to put him on the prayer list."

Autumn threw her forearm across her forehead. "A lot of good that will do. We pray for the unit every Sunday. Look what it's gotten us. Josh hurt. Dad missing or..." She sobbed. "Or worse."

Emily stroked her arm. "Hey, you don't know that."

"And you don't know, either. I checked my email. Nothing."

Drew moved over next to Emily and squeezed her shoulder. "Lying there thinking the worst isn't going to help."

Emily turned her head and glared at him. Did he think he was making things better? Autumn was really hurting. Her anger dissolved when she saw the sheen of compassion in his eyes. It was easier to be angry with Drew than face her fears about Neal.

"Come on," he coaxed. "Take Emily's hand and say a prayer with us. You'll feel better."

Autumn rolled away from them toward the computer. "No, take yourselves and your useless prayers and go."

Emily touched her.

"Go. I mean it."

Lifting her hand took far more effort than any weight training she'd ever done at the gym.

"Okay. I'll check in on you later."

"Don't bother, unless you hear from Daddy."

Emily blinked back tears as she rose and walked across the room. She turned and looked back. Drew still stood by the bed with his hands stuffed in the front pockets of his jeans, staring at Autumn's back. She creaked the door open to get his attention. After a final glance at her niece, he followed her out.

"We shouldn't have pushed her," Emily said when they reached the end of the hall out of earshot.

"Or we should have pushed harder. She's tearing herself apart with worry. Praying would have lifted her spirit."

"I can understand her wanting to be alone. She's scared and feels betrayed."

"Prayer would help."

"She may be more private with her faith, like me. You're pushing her away from God instead of letting her turn to Him when she's ready."

He pressed his lips together and shook his head. "Are you going back down to finish cleaning the cabin? I don't think she should be alone."

"No, I'm going to work on my ad campaign. The cleaning is too mindless. I need to do something that will keep me from thinking about everything."

"That's what I mean. It would help Autumn if she was doing something. You should see if you can get her to help you finish up later, so it will be done before your renters arrive."

Emily rubbed her temples. They'd have to take what they got. She'd lost all of her earlier joy in making the cabins ready and seeing her parent's regular vacationers. "I'll see. Don't you need to get back to the camp?"

He frowned. "Right. I'll probably pick up dinner there, too." He turned when he reached the doorway to the kitchen. "You know where to reach me if you need to."

She stayed in the living room until she heard the outside door click closed behind him. Then she sank into the overstuffed couch and closed her eyes. Her frustration with Autumn and Drew drained away, allowing her worry about Neal to overwhelm her. The ticking of the clock on the opposite wall told her how alone she was. She knew Drew had been trying to help. If only his helpfulness hadn't been so irritating.

"Lord," Emily started, at a loss as to what to say next. "Just make everything all right."

Autumn seemed a little better the next day. She got herself up and off to work at the camp. Neither of them said anything to each other about Neal. Emily threw herself into finishing the cabins and called the chimney sweep about the cabins and the fireplace stove in the house. After lunch, she tried to lose herself in her computer design work, but found herself checking for new email often.

The ring of the doorbell a couple of hours later paralyzed her. No one used the doorbell. Heart pounding, she went to the front door. Relief flooded her when she saw that the uniform the man at the door wore was a delivery person uniform. A bright yellow truck with a spray of flowers was parked at the end of the stone walkway.

She pulled open the door. He was holding an enormous vase of deep red roses.

"I have a delivery for Emily Hazard."

"That's me."

"Either someone loves you a lot or owes you a big apology." The delivery person grinned.

Emily reached for the roses, hoping to use them to hide the blush she felt creeping up her neck.

"Do I need to sign anything?" She'd never gotten a flower delivery before.

"No, that's it. Enjoy." He returned to his truck.

Emily carried the roses to the kitchen and placed them on the counter. She smiled to herself as she lifted the card from the plastic holder nestled among the flowers.

Sorry about yesterday. Drew.

She pressed the card to her chest and leaned forward to breathe in their scent.

"Is it safe for me to come in?"

Emily started and the card fluttered to the floor.

"Yes, it's safe for you to come in."

Drew closed the distance between the door and Emily and scooped up the card. He presented it to her with a flourish. "Do you like them?"

"They're beautiful. Red are my favorite."

"I guessed that."

"Have I told you how spooky that is?"

"A time or two." He drew her to him. Soothing warmth infused her head to toes.

She laid her head against his chest. His heart thumped in alternate time with hers. They stood silently in each others arms until the beats reached a regular rhythm.

Drew broke the silence. "Did you hear anything?"

She shook her head against his chest, seeking his warmth to counter the chill of fear his question awakened. "How was Autumn today? I only saw her for a minute this morning before she went to work."

"She seemed okay. A little quieter than usual."

The crunching sound of someone walking up the gravel driveway pulled them apart.

Autumn breezed through the screen door. "Hi." She dumped her backpack on the counter by the door and handed Emily a couple of bills from the mailbox. "Jack and I are going to go out bowling or something. He'll be by as soon as he gets out of work and cleaned up." She disappeared upstairs.

"That seemed pretty normal," Emily said.

"Yeah, she probably needed time to get things in perspective. It's not like Neal can email or call her every day. I have a few more things to take care of at the camp before I call it a day. Do you want to do something tonight since Autumn will be out?"

She didn't want to go anywhere. What if Neal called? "Why don't we stay in and watch a movie?"

"Fine by me. See you in an hour or so."

A few minutes later, Autumn came back downstairs, her shorts and camp T-shirt exchanged for jeans and a tank top covered with a three-quarter sleeved sweatshirt jacket. She rummaged around in the cupboard and came up with a granola bar.

"Are you going to be here for dinner?"

"No, we'll get something out." She unwrapped the bar and inhaled it.

"You okay?" Emily asked the million-dollar question.

Autumn crumpled the wrapper and tossed it in the trash container. "As okay as I can be, I guess."

"Do you want to talk about it?"

Something flickered in Autumn's eyes. She lowered her gaze to the floor.

"I won't be pushy and stuff about praying like Drew was."

"He was okay. You guys prayed for Dad, right?"

"I've been praying as hard as I can that we hear from him soon."

"You *and* Drew," the teen pressed.

"I'm sure he has been, too."

"Not together?"

"It doesn't matter whether we pray alone or together. God still listens."

"Then what do we have church for?"

Exasperation ticked Emily's temperature up. Yesterday Autumn had said that congregational prayer was useless. "Fellowship, praise, guidance, support."

"I know. Sorry. I'm frustrated and scared."

Emily gave her a big hug. "Me, too. Me, too."

Chapter Fourteen

Emily sat up on the living room couch and rubbed the crick in her neck. She squinted out the bright morning sun to read the clock on the DVR. Eight thirty-five. Drew had left at midnight, when their movie ended. She'd still been wide-awake and decided to wait up for Autumn, who was supposed to be home by midnight—Neal's rules. The last time Emily had checked the clock, it had been two-thirty.

I wonder what time she slipped in and how she got by me.

Emily's mother had always awoken the minute she or Neal had walked in the house, no matter how late or quiet they'd tried to be. Her throat clogged. *He was all right. He had to be all right.* She channeled her fears into anger at Autumn. She might be a week away from moving out, but she was still under Emily's watch. And they'd come so far over the summer. She stood and rotated her head side to side. Might as well go wake Autumn up for church.

"Autumn." Emily knocked on the bedroom door. "Time for church." When she received no answer and didn't hear any stirring, she knocked again louder before turning the doorknob and pushing the door open. The room was empty, Autumn's bed hadn't been slept in. Emily's heart dropped. Autumn hadn't come home.

Halfway down the stairs, anger pushed back Emily's fear. As she stomped into the kitchen, she saw Jack through the window in the door to the garage.

"Where is she?" Emily had the words out as quickly as she opened the door. She looked around Jack and at his car. It looked empty.

He shifted his weight from one foot to the other. "I don't know. I was hoping she was here. That's why I came. She was really upset when I left."

"Left where? You left her alone? The way she was feeling?"

"The diner. No. We stopped for coffee after bowling. I got a call for the tow truck. Someone had a breakdown on the highway. I'm on call this weekend. They were gone when I got back."

"Who was gone?"

He jerked back. She shouldn't take her angry frustration out on him. Even if he'd left Autumn at the diner by herself, she would have been fine. People there knew her. It was one of the good things about Paradox. People looked out for each other. But why didn't she call for a ride home if she needed one?

"Autumn and Jule and Ezra and some friend of his from college. I called Autumn's cell phone when I finished the tow, but it went right to voice mail."

Emily had called Autumn, too, several times, and hadn't gotten through, either. She'd thought it was the spotty cell coverage in the mountains. Apprehension gripped her.

"What about Jule? Did she come home? Did you talk with her before you came over here?"

"She must have come home. She and Mom and Dad were going up to Grandma's to go to church with her and celebrate her birthday. I couldn't go, since I'm on call, covering for Dad. They were gone when I got up, and I haven't been able to get through to them, either. But if Jule hadn't come home, I would have heard about it. Loud and clear."

She released her pent-up breath with a whoosh. "Autumn must have gone with Jule and your parents."

Jack dropped his gaze to the top stair. "I don't know. Like I said, she was really upset. Maybe you should look at this." He handed her an envelope. "It came to Autumn at our house. She left it in my car."

"Come in." She took the envelope and sat down at the table. *Autumn Hazard care of Jule Hill* at the Hill's address was scrawled across the front. The postmark was San Antonio, but there was no return address. Her stomach clenched and she offered a small plea to heaven for strength and guidance as she removed the sheet of paper from the envelope.

A murky haze clouded her vision as she read the terse message:

> *Don't contact me again. I'm not your mother. I gave up that responsibility when I left Paradox eighteen years ago. And I'm not about to take it up again now.*
> *Vanessa Edwards*

Autumn's mother. Poor Autumn. Emily laid her head on the table to stop the spinning.

"Drew," a disembodied voice said. "You've got to get up here fast."

Someone, Jack, touched her shoulder. "Are you okay? Can I get you water or something?"

She lifted her head. Jack's face was twisted in panic. "Yes, water."

The kitchen door burst open. "What happened?" Drew asked.

"I thought she was fainting or something," Jack said.

"Emily?" Drew's eyes were clouded with concern.

"I'm okay." Her shaky voice belied her statement.

He pulled a chair next to her, sat down and put his arm across the back of her chair.

"Take a look." She pointed at the letter.

Drew whistled.

"Autumn got it yesterday, sent to her at Jack and Jule's house."

He picked up the paper and tossed it down again. "I never should have mailed that letter for her."

"And she didn't come home last night." Emily brushed a tear from her cheek and buried her face in Drew's chest.

The phone rang. "Please Lord, let that be Autumn," she whispered against the soft cotton.

She pulled away from Drew. A chill ran through her when she broke contact. "Hello."

"May I speak with Emily Hazard? This is Officer Dibble of the Plattsburgh Police Department."

"This is she." The chill turned into a paralyzing freeze.

"Are you the guardian of the minor, Autumn Hazard?"

"Yes," she choked out.

"You'll need to come to the station. She's being held for unlawful possession of alcohol."

"What?" She braced herself against the wall.

"Do you need directions?"

"Yes, please." She jotted down the information the officer gave her on the pad on the counter next to the phone.

She hung up the phone and faced the guys. "I'm going to kill her. Autumn is at the police station in Plattsburgh. They picked her up for underage drinking."

"But Autumn doesn't drink," Jack blurted.

His outburst did little to reassure her. The letter from her mother…no, the woman who gave birth to her. Vanessa was no mother. The letter on top of her worry about her dad might have sent her over the edge.

"I need to drive up and get her." She grabbed the keys to Neal's truck from the counter where she'd left them.

Small-Town Sweethearts

Drew lifted them from her hand. "*We* need to go get her."

"Thanks." His support gave her a welcome jolt of relief. Call her a coward, but she had no desire to face the police or Autumn alone. More than ever, she could see why it took two people to raise a child.

"Uh, I guess I'll go home."

Emily and Drew stared at Jack as if they'd forgotten he was there.

"You do that," Drew said.

Jack cringed at Drew's harsh tone, and Emily felt badly for the guy. He really was pretty much just the messenger. Jack hightailed it out of the house and, by the time Drew had backed Neal's truck out of the garage, the teen was speeding up the road.

"Wasn't Autumn supposed to be with Jack last night?" Drew shoved the gearshift into first. "What was he thinking letting her take off to Plattsburgh?" He jammed the transmission through the next three gears to fifth and hit cruising speed in record time. "Why wasn't he with her? He knew she was upset."

"He couldn't. He had to go in to work." She couldn't believe she was defending Jack to Drew. "He was on call and had to go tow someone. And it's not like he left her all alone. She was with Jule."

"Granted, that's a problem with work. It doesn't always lend itself to personal situations."

She was too wrapped up with Autumn and what she was going to do with her when they got to Plattsburgh to try to decipher that cryptic statement. She sat silent for a while watching the trees wiz by. "Did you?" Her thoughts came out in a half-formed question.

"Did I what?"

"Drink when you were in high school or college?"

His eyebrows lifted and the corner of his mouth smirked up. "What do you think?"

"I went to a party or two in college. But Autumn is only seventeen."

"For a couple more weeks, and Jack says she doesn't drink."

"True." But that didn't make her feel any better. Worse, really. The devastation Autumn must be feeling was enough to make anyone act out of character. They rode the next hour of the way to Plattsburgh in charged silence.

"I need the directions to the police station," Drew said when they reached the city limits.

Emily read them and Drew maneuvered the city streets to the station on the banks of the Saranac River. He parked the truck in the small lot and opened her door. After inhaling and exhaling a deep breath, she stepped out. They walked from the parking lot of the low nondescript stone building to the main entrance. Drew held open the glass door and Emily went in. An officer sat at a high glassed-in counter. Cameras were strategically placed around the whitewashed room and rounded mirrors shined down from all four corners.

She stepped up to the counter and spoke into a microphone. "I'm Emily Hazard, here to pick up Autumn Hazard."

"ID?"

Emily dug into her bag for her wallet and fumbled through it to find her driver's license. She slid it through the opening in the glass.

The officer studied the license. "Sit over there." He motioned to a row of molded plastic chairs bolted to the floor against the wall. "And you are?" he asked Drew.

Drew handed him his ready license. "I'm with her."

"Lucky you," he said dryly as he handed the license back.

After an interminable ten minutes, a buzzer sounded, and another officer brought Autumn into the waiting area. She scuffed over to them head down, her hair falling over her face.

"Autumn, honey," Emily said.

The teen pushed her hair back and slowly made eye contact with Emily. Her eyes were red rimmed with mascara streaked down to her cheeks.

"Aunt Jinx," she sobbed. "I...I..."

Emily opened her arms and the officer let Autumn propel herself into them. Emily held her as the officer spoke.

"We're not charging her. She passed the breathalyzer test, and didn't have any illegal substances on her. You need to sign the paperwork at the desk."

"Thank you."

"She's lucky. You're lucky. This time." He looked from Emily to Drew and back. "But you need to keep a tighter leash on her. You look like nice people. A lot of the people at this party were not." He dismissed them with a nod.

Emily unwound herself from Autumn and took care of the paperwork. She held her tongue until the door to the police station was firmly shut behind her. "What were you thinking?"

Autumn shrugged.

"I was so worried." She motioned to Drew. "We were so worried. Jack's worried. He was over to the house first thing this morning."

A couple of guys on the sidewalk across the street looked over.

"Let's talk in the truck," Drew said as he unlocked the vehicle.

Autumn climbed in back. "I'm sorry." Her voice wavered.

Emily turned around as far as she could in the front seat to face her.

"I had a really bad day. I got a letter." She swallowed. "A letter from—"

Emily softened. "I know. Jack showed it to me."

"I don't want to talk about it. I didn't need her before. I don't need her now." She spat out the words.

"We can talk about it later when you're ready."

"That'll be, like, never. I never want to hear her name again."

"All right." For now. "So, how did you end up in Plattsburgh by yourself?"

"We were at the diner deciding what we wanted to do. Ezra had a friend with him who said some of their friends from college were having a party. I thought it would be a good way to forget everything for a while."

Emily made a mental note to tell Jule's mother what the officer had said about Ezra's college friends. She was turning into a busybody. But Mrs. Hill would want to know. Emily knew that. She wouldn't be insinuating herself into someone else's life. Emily cared about Jule. Like the people at church and others in Paradox that she'd always complained about had cared about her. She just hadn't seen it that way.

"Then, Jack got that stupid work call and couldn't go. If he wasn't going, Jule didn't think she should go. And Ezra wasn't going if Jule didn't go. It's his last weekend before he goes back to college."

Drew interrupted. "So, you took off with some guy you didn't know. Not smart."

"Drew!" Emily touched his arm. His muscles corded under her fingertips.

"No, Aunt Jinx. He's right. It was stupid. Ezra's friend ditched me shortly after we got there. I didn't know anyone. It was awful. I kept trying to call Jack, but I couldn't get through. I hoped he'd come for me anyway. Then the cops came."

Emily's heart went out to Autumn, as if the teen hadn't felt abandoned enough before. But maybe last night was just what she needed to grow up a little. After all, in a week she and Jule were going to be off on their own—more or less.

"We're glad you're okay," Drew said gruffly. "Hope you learned a lesson."

For some reason, Drew vocalizing her thought irritated

her. Autumn was her responsibility, not Drew's. "Jack said he tried to reach you all night and your phone kept going directly to voice mail." Maybe that would make Autumn feel a little better.

"You mean he doesn't hate me?"

"No, he doesn't hate you. He was really worried. No one hates you."

"Except my mother." The last word dripped with venom.

"No, she doesn't. She doesn't even know you."

"She doesn't even want to."

Drew gripped the steering wheel tighter and waited to see how Emily fielded this one.

Autumn suddenly squealed and he swerved onto the shoulder of the highway. "What?"

"It's Daddy. He's okay. He emailed me." Autumn waved her cell phone over the back of the seat. "He says they've been kind of busy."

An understatement, for sure. Who knew what Neal had been through the past couple of days or what he may have had to go through to get his message to Autumn. He sure hoped she appreciated it.

"And he wants to know if we've heard anything about Josh."

"I'll check with Pastor Joel when we get home and let him know," Emily said. "You probably shouldn't say anything about the letter."

"I'm not stupid."

"Of course not." The corners of Emily's mouth twitched as if she were fighting a smile.

"I'm going to text Jack and let him know," Autumn said.

No more concern about Jack hating her? Were women of all ages so changeable? But this was harmless, nothing like the turnaround his ex-fiancée pulled on him when he'd lost his job. He didn't live up to her expectations of marrying a

Wall Street up-and-comer, and she couldn't marry someone who wasn't her financial and social equal. He glanced sideways at Emily and shifted in his seat. Emily had expectations, too. She expected him to return to New York for work when camp ended.

Emily broke his thought. "Don't make any plans," she started. "You're—"

"I know," Autumn said. "Grounded. I'm too tired to care. I'm going right to bed when we get home, probably until tomorrow morning."

"We'll talk when you wake up."

He wasn't sure how Emily was going to take this, but he had to say it. "You should talk with Pastor Joel about your mother."

Emily's mouth went tight. "What? And have the whole town know our family business?"

"He could recommend someone Autumn could talk to."

"It's a small town," Emily said as if that explained everything, "You've never lived in a small town."

"What am I doing now if not living in a small town?" Drew asked. Emily needed to see the community realistically through adult eyes, not from her teenage perspective.

"Slumming until a real job comes along in the city."

"Hardly." He was working hard to make the camp season successful. But the *real job* reference hit home. He hadn't heard any more from Scott about the coalition getting the funding to make the camp year-round. So, the way things were looking, he probably would have to leave Paradox Lake after camp was over for a job somewhere else.

"Stop! Both of you. Jinx is right that you probably don't know how vicious the local gossips can be or how much they seem to know about everyone's business. But you're right about Pastor. He'd never share anything told to him in confidence. I may go talk with him."

"Good."

Emily didn't say anything.

"Now, I'd tell you to hug and make up, but you're driving and I've had enough excitement and police contact to last me a good long time."

"Amen to that," Emily said.

"So, why don't you go to the county fair tonight to forget about me and all the stuff I put you through? I hear they have a great bluegrass band there."

Drew looked over at Emily. Her expression had softened.

"I've always loved the fair," she said.

"See. Take her to the fair as a make-up date. She loves the fair."

"I might just do that," Drew said.

"Yoo-hoo. I'm right here, you know," Emily said.

With the breeze from the open window ruffling her hair and filling the truck cab with the subtle citrus scent of her shampoo, he was all too aware of that fact. "Do you want go to the fair?"

"I'd really like to go."

His pulse picked up.

"But not tonight. You can't seriously think I'd leave Autumn at the house alone."

He hadn't thought of that.

"I won't go anywhere," Autumn said. "Or have anyone in. You can take the truck keys."

Drew's guard went up. Autumn was starting to sound a little too much like him and Scott trying to put something over on their mother.

Emily's face turned a little gray. "Grounding aside, I don't think it's a good idea for you to be alone tonight. You've been through a lot the past couple of days."

He hadn't even thought about that aspect of leaving Autumn alone. "Wait. I have an idea. Jamie owes me for the extra half day off I gave her for her RN continuing education seminar and for watching Rose and Opal so she could go.

She can bring Myles and the girls up and stay at the house. The girls are crazy about Autumn, and Jamie says Myles is suffering a bad case of computer withdrawal. If it's okay for him to use one of your computers."

Autumn groaned.

The idea was sounding better and better.

"But isn't Jamie on call if one of the campers gets sick or hurt?" Emily asked.

"The house is nearly as close to the campers' cabins as her cabin is, and she'd have her cell phone with her if one of the counselors needed to reach her."

"I suppose. Autumn would be in good hands, too, with Jamie being a nurse and all, if she got feeling really down."

"Aunt Jinx, I'm not going to do anything to myself. Daddy's okay. I wouldn't even if he wasn't."

"You're sure? You'll be okay with Jamie?"

"Ye-es, although I'd be better without the chatterbugs."

Up all night, a couple hours of sleep and an invasion by a very busy four- and six-year-old. Sounded to him just what Autumn needed after what she'd put Emily through.

"I do love the fair, and I haven't been in years." Emily's statement ended with a note of wistfulness.

He didn't know why going to the fair tonight had taken on such great importance to him. But it had.

Chapter Fifteen

"Autumn, Autumn, Autumn. We're here!" Jamie's daughters Rose and Opal raced across the room to the stairway. "We brought our *Little Mermaid* DVD," they called up the stairs.

"Girls," their mother warned, as their older brother Myles rolled his eyes.

"Let them go," Emily said.

Jamie started after the two. "But from what Drew said, Autumn is one tired girl."

"Yep, and a little pain for what she put us through won't hurt." Emily searched Jamie's face for clues as to how much of the situation Drew had shared with her. The woman wasn't a local, so she wouldn't be tied into the local grapevine. Still, Emily was uncomfortable with Drew's openness with her family matters.

"Grounding isn't enough? Autumn must have really done it this time."

There. That's what she meant, although it sounded like Drew hadn't given Jamie the details. But that could be worse. Who knew what Jamie might be thinking?

"Hey, is this a private conversation or can anyone join in?" Emily hadn't heard Drew come in, and since when was anything private? She chided herself again for her attitude. In her current mood, maybe the fair wasn't such a good idea. And the appreciative look that Jamie gave Drew all decked out in softly faded jeans and a polo shirt didn't sweeten Emily's disposition.

"Ready?" The warmth of his smile softened her irritation.

"I like your hair like that," he said.

She'd left her hair down with the sides drawn back into a barrette. Drew lifted his hand and smoothed an errant curl back from her forehead. His finger drifted down along the line of her jaw. Emily's breath caught at his touch and the living room seemed void of oxygen.

"Uh. I'll just go check on Autumn and the girls." Jamie slipped away unnoticed.

He leaned down and pressed his lips to hers.

"What was that for?" she asked, missing the heat of his nearness as soon as his lips left hers.

"Because you're too beautiful to resist." His pupils grew wider as he held her gaze with his.

"I see."

"We'd better get going."

"Yes, we should." She made no effort to move.

"Are you going to watch *The Little Mermaid* with us," a high-pitched voice piped up behind them. Rose.

"Autumn is going to make us popcorn," her sister Opal added. "Maybe she'll let you have some, too."

"Like I said. Time to get going." Drew stepped away from her.

"No, honey. We have to go. You can tell Drew all about the movie tomorrow."

"Thanks," he said under his breath.

"Aw, we've seen it before," Rose said.

"About six times," Opal chimed in. "So, we could tell you now."

"Sorry, squirt, but we can't stay. I don't want to ruin your girls' night out."

The little towhead screwed up her face as if she were thinking hard. "You're a boy. But she's not." Opal pointed at Emily. "She could stay."

"But she's *my* girl."

Emily's knees went weak at his simple statement. Was she? She caught a glimmer in his eyes. He was simply stating things so that they would make sense to Opal, and here she was reacting like a lovelorn teen with her first boyfriend.

"Yeah, she's his girlfriend," her older sister explained. "And they have to have date night out like when Daddy comes home on leave. That's what boyfriends and girlfriends do." She stood feet splayed, arms akimbo, obviously an expert on boyfriends and girlfriends.

"That's right," Drew said. "I'll talk with you two tomorrow at lunch, and you can tell me all about *The Little Mermaid*."

Emily smiled at how well Drew and the little girls got along. "I'll see you later," she said to Jamie and Autumn, who had come downstairs with them. "You're okay with us going?"

"Ye-es." The way Autumn stretched out the word clearly said she thought she'd be even better without Jamie's and the girls' supervision.

"All right, then."

"Thanks again," Drew said to Jamie as he whisked Emily out the door and off to the fairgrounds.

The smell of animals and aroma of fried foods of every description hung on the breeze as Emily and Drew walked down the midway of the fair. Fingers twined in his, she watched the young couples all around them. Painful memories filled her head. She'd never come to the fair with a boy, a teenage rite in Paradox. As a younger teen, she'd come with her best friend from elementary school. But Mandy had moved away their sophomore year, and Emily had skipped the fair after that, despite how much she liked it. What teen wanted to go to the fair—or anywhere, for that matter—with her parents?

She gripped Drew's hand a little tighter. He smiled at her and chased away the bad memories.

"Cotton candy!" She pointed at a vendor spinning a cloud of pink around a paper cone.

"Don't tell me you want some."

"Why not?" she challenged him.

Drew studied her as if she'd grown a second head. "Uh, you do know what's in those? Nothing but sugar and chemicals."

"I can't eat healthy all of the time. It's…" She searched for the right word. "It's un-American."

"Well, one certainly wouldn't want to be un-American at a county fair." He paid the vendor for one cone and handed it to Emily.

"None for you?" She pulled off a tuff and stuffed it in her mouth. It melted into sweet nothingness.

"No, I'll share yours." He pinched off a small amount, hesitated a moment and put it in his mouth. "Ummm," he feigned.

"If you don't like it, you don't have to eat it. More for me." She pulled off another tuff.

"Watch out."

Drew took her elbow and guided her out of the way of the trunk of a giant purple elephant carried by a young woman whose adoring eyes were much more on her companion than where she was walking. Emily eyed the stuffed animal. The woman's boyfriend must have won it for her at one of the game booths. An old longing she obviously hadn't buried deep enough filled her. Not that she'd ever really wanted one of the gaudy fair prizes, but she'd always been a little jealous of the girls whose boyfriends had won them one.

Drew whistled. "I haven't seen one of those since I was a kid."

A large purple elephant? Emily thought, her gaze still on the young couple.

"I figured they'd been banned under some safety law or another."

She craned her neck to see around the crowd to see what he was looking at.

"Mom said it was a waste of good money."

"What are you talking about?"

"The darts. I'm going to give it a try. I used to be in a dart league at church."

Her heart raced with the repressed teenage longing. Maybe he would win her something.

"Cheer me on." He stepped up to the booth, paid his money and got a handful of darts.

"Break three balloons, get any prize on the bottom shelf," the hawker said. "Break five balloons, get any prize on the middle shelf. Break all seven balloons, get a top shelf prize."

Drew threw his first dart. And missed. He connected with the second one, but the next two missed. Another hit and miss. One dart left. Emily rocked on her heals. She'd be happy with a small prize.

Drew's last dart missed.

She buried her disappointment. "That's okay. The games are rigged, you know."

"Yeah, I know. Let's stick around. I want to watch a couple people play. See what works."

"Sure, why not. The night's young."

Drew viewed the next player from the right and the second player from the left. After monitoring a third person from behind, the hawker barked at him, "Play or leave."

"Play." Drew handed over the money and took his darts. The first throw arched up and came down and punctured two balloons. Shots two and three missed. Four knocked out another balloon.

Emily clapped. Drew had won a small prize, even if he didn't pop any more balloons.

He tossed five and six and brought his tally up to five.

Emily eyed the prizes on the second shelf.

Drew stepped back and studied the two remaining balloons.

"Don't take all night," the man in the booth said in a low tone only Drew and Emily could hear. "People are waiting."

A crowd *had* gathered around the booth, but more to watch Drew, Emily guessed, than to play.

Drew took another moment before throwing another shot that arched up and came down through the two remaining balloons.

"And the man wins a top-shelf prize," the man said. "What will it be?"

Drew smiled at Emily. "Your choice."

"The photo. The one on the left of the midway."

The man took the picture from the shelf and handed it to her.

"No one's ever won me a prize before." She touched the glass. "I'll always have it as a reminder of today."

"I'm glad I was the first."

Emily laughed. She was, too.

"What next?" he asked, slipping his arm around her waist.

"The animal and 4-H exhibit tents."

"Seriously?"

"Seriously." She nodded. "You haven't been to a county fair if you haven't seen the exhibits."

"If you say so."

She guided him into the first tent.

When they came out of the last exhibit tent, the first stars of the evening were appearing in the blue-black sky.

"My choice now," Drew said. "The Ferris wheel."

"Fine with me, as long you don't rock the seat when we stop at the top."

"Sure."

"Promise?"

"Promise."

"Okay, let's do it."

Drew bought tickets for the ride, then they waited their turn in line. When they reached the front of the line, Drew held the seat while she climbed in. Once they were both seated and the safety bar closed, he wrapped his arm around her shoulders and pulled her close. She rested her head on his shoulder.

As the ride circled up and down, Emily didn't know if the exhilaration rushing through her was from the ride or her proximity to Drew. The evening had been perfect, better than any of her teenage fantasies of a date at the fair. The Ferris wheel slowed and started making its stop and start release of passengers. Emily and Drew's seat inched its way toward the top.

"Look at the stars," he said. "You can't see them like this in New York."

Emily murmured an agreement, admiring the lines of his profile as he pointed to the sky more than the stars. Her heart quickened.

The Ferris wheel lurched to another stop with their car at the top. The car jerked and swung.

Emily glared at Drew.

"Not me. I'm a man of my word."

She relaxed, and the ride started up again, only to come to a jarring halt with a loud clang.

After a minute, she asked, "Can you see what's going on? I don't want to look down, and don't rock, okay?" She hated showing her fear of heights.

Drew looked over his side of the car. "The operator is on the phone. Looks like a problem."

A cool breeze blew over them, and Emily shivered more than the coolness warranted.

A half an hour later after another announcement from the ride operator that they would have them down as quickly as possible, she gingerly slipped her cell phone from her tightly clutched purse. "I'm going to call home and let Jamie know we may be late, and she can put the girls to sleep in the extra bed in my room."

"Good idea."

Autumn answered the phone. "Hi, Aunt Jinx."

"Hi. Can you put Jamie on?…What do you mean, she's not there?" From the look on his face, Drew shared her outrage.

"Oh, okay…No, I'll talk to her when we get home. We're stuck at the top of the Ferris wheel, so it may be a while. Bye."

"Did one of the campers get sick?" Drew asked.

"No, my mother is there."

The conflicting feelings of relief that her mother was here to help with Autumn, and disappointment that Mom thought she needed help, gave a certain appeal to being stuck atop the Ferris wheel a while longer.

Chapter Sixteen

Drew walked Emily up to the house from the truck.

"I had a nice time," she said.

"Good." He smiled. "I wasn't sure. You were awfully quiet on the drive back."

"Sorry. It's just that my parents could have trusted me to handle Autumn. I don't know how Mom even found out about Plattsburgh. That *has* to be why she came back without telling me."

"Maybe Mrs. Hill called her after Autumn talked with Jack," Drew said.

Emily nodded. "Probably."

She wanted to be mad. But she was sure that if Mrs. Hill had called Mom, she'd meant well. She scuffed her toe against the porch.

When she looked up. Drew was looking at her, his eyes soft.

"Uh." He cleared his throat. "I'd better get going. Morning comes early at camp."

"Okay. Good night."

Emily watched him walk to his truck. Was that the end to their awesome night? She tripped over the door threshold and her fair photo flew out of her hand onto the kitchen floor. She picked it up to see a long crack across the glass covering. A sign that it was time for her to go back to New York?

"Jinx, is that you?" Her mother met her at the living room doorway.

"Hi, Mom." She hugged her. "You didn't have to rush up here because of Autumn. I have everything under control."

"That's not why I came." She motioned for her to sit on the couch. "I was so upset after you called about Neal yesterday, that I wanted to be with you and Autumn in case you needed me."

Tears moistened Emily's eyes.

"Your dad suggested I fly up, to get me out of his hair, I think. You know how I go into hypercleaning mode when I'm anxious about something."

"I know, and Grandma's condo isn't that big. Dad would have no place to escape."

"Exactly. It's too wretchedly hot in August there for him to go outside. You didn't get my email about coming?"

"No, I haven't checked my mailbox all day. Autumn told you about Neal? He's fine." Guilt washed over Emily. She'd been so tied up with Autumn and her excitement about the fair that she'd never gotten back to her mom about Neal.

"Oh, yes. I got Autumn's text when I got off the plane."

"How did you get here from the airport?"

"A rental car. I let the woman who was here with Autumn drive it down to the lake."

"Jamie." Typical Mom, letting a woman she didn't know drive off with her rental car.

"Don't look at me like that. You wouldn't have had anyone who wasn't trustworthy stay with Autumn, not after what she'd been through."

"Thanks, Mom. She told you?"

"Enough of it. Anyway, Jamie's little girls were so tired.

Too tired to walk back. They are so cute, aren't they? The older one reminds me a little bit of Autumn at that age."

"Yes, they are sweet." She geared up for one of her mother's not-so-subtle hints about more grandchildren.

"How was your date? I remember how much you always liked the fair."

Better than a press for grandchildren, although the question made Emily feel like a teenager home from her first date. But in a good way. As a teen, she would have thought her mother prying, rather than caring as she did now.

She told her about their evening, right down to being stranded for an hour on the Ferris wheel.

"We had a really good time." Or at least she had, remembering Drew's abrupt departure. Had there been too much family stuff for him for one day? Her heart lightened. Once she and Drew were back at work in New York, it would be less of an issue.

"He won me this." She showed her the fair photo. "I tripped and dropped it when I came in."

"Oh." Her mother traced the crack in the glass. "I think I have another frame just that size. I'll get it out tomorrow. So, you like him."

Emily laughed. "Yes, I like him."

Her mother smiled. Fortunately, she knew when to stop. "When we talked the other day, I was too upset to tell you our news. Your father has talked your grandmother into selling the condo and moving back here with us. He's already put the condo on the market furnished and hired someone to pack and ship any of his mother's things they can't fit in the car. They hope to be here the end of next week."

"That soon?"

"You know your father when he makes up his mind to do something."

"Yeah."

"Gee, don't sound so happy about it." Her mother's sarcasm snapped her from the melancholy that was settling over her.

"It's just that with you and Dad and Grandma here, I don't really need to stay through the end of the month. I could go back to my place in the city. The people who were subletting moved out this past weekend."

"But you don't have to go. We have plenty of room, especially with Autumn moving into her apartment. She told me she and Jule want to move in next week so they can be all settled before their classes start. You've already arranged with your work to be here. Stay. We haven't had a good visit in a long time."

"I'd like that. A lot."

Mom was right. As much as Emily thought she needed to get back to work at the agency office in New York City, a little R & R with her family first was more important.

"They should be here by now, shouldn't they?" Mom fretted.

"I'm sure they'll be here soon, and if you wipe the stove down one more time, it won't have any enamel left on it."

"The sauce spattered." A crunch of tires on the driveway sent her mother to the window. "It's Drew. I invited him for dinner."

Of course she had. Mom had had Drew to the house for one thing or another every day since she'd arrived last week.

He knocked once at the door and walked in. "They're not here yet?"

Emily laughed.

"What's that about?"

"Mom's been saying that every two minutes for the last forty-five minutes."

"I have not."

The sound of another car stopped Emily from having to

disagree with her mother. She beat her mother to the window. "It's Dad and Grandma."

Her mother was out the door almost before Emily finished. She and Drew followed. Her father stepped from the car and hugged her mother before helping her grandmother out. She marveled at how close her parents still were after thirty-six years of marriage. Her gaze slid to Drew. She forced it back to her grandmother standing next to the car.

"Grandma." Emily hugged her.

"Emily. It's been too long. You never did get down to Florida to visit me. And this must be your young man."

Emily groaned silently. "This is Drew Stacey. He's the manager of the church camp at the lake this summer. My grandmother, Evelyn Hazard."

"Drew." She offered him her hand. "Ted has told me a lot about you and your camp."

"Nice to meet you, Mrs. Hazard. Can I get your luggage for you?"

"Thank you. Ted's tired. He wouldn't let me do any of the driving."

"Not that tired, Mom. I'll give you a hand, Drew."

The three women went inside and sat around the kitchen table.

"I'm so glad to be back at the lake," Grandma Hazard said. "It really was your grandfather's idea to sell our house here and live in Florida year-round. Until Ted and Mary came down to help me after my stroke, I'd forgotten how much I'd missed the lake and the mountains."

"It is beautiful here, especially in the summer," Emily agreed.

The door swung open and the guys came in loaded down with luggage. "Where do you want Mom's stuff?" Ted asked.

"Put it in Emily's room."

They headed down the hall.

"Would you like some iced tea, Grandma? Mom?" Emily

got the pitcher of tea from the refrigerator and poured them each a tall glass.

Drew and Emily's father returned a minute later. "If dinner isn't right away, I'd like to go down to the lake with Drew and see what he's done."

"Autumn won't be here until six, so you have a half hour."

"Got it. We'll be back."

"I can't believe Autumn is old enough to have her own apartment," Grandma said as they left. "Of course, I was married, for all of a month, when I was her age."

The older woman sipped her tea. "Emily, I can take Autumn's room upstairs. I don't want to put you out."

"No, Grandma. You should have the downstairs bedroom. You're not putting me out. I'll be going back to New York in a couple weeks."

"What about your friend, Drew?"

Emily wasn't sure where her grandmother was headed with her question. Her mother's placid expression didn't give her any clue. "He'll be closing the camp and going back to New York, too."

"I was sure Ted said Drew was staying in Paradox."

Emily's heart stopped.

"I do get things confused sometimes," Grandma mused. "I don't always hear as well as I did."

Emily's mother pressed her lips together in a thin line.

Emily brushed off the sinking feeling that they knew something she didn't. Grandma must be confused, and Mom was concerned about her. Drew's job at the camp was temporary. His real life was in New York, like hers. As much as he liked the Adirondacks, he couldn't seriously be considering staying here.

Could he?

Chapter Seventeen

The sparrows chirped a lively song in the trees above her as Emily walked a message for Drew down to him at the lodge the next day. The phone call for Drew from the New York investment bank human resources director had been a welcome interruption. Maybe the exercise would brighten her spirits. Her work hadn't been going well, and she was in a funk. Emily picked up her pace and rubbed the paper with the return phone number between her thumb and finger. The message could mean a job offer for Drew.

Drew heard the light knock on the half-open door of his office and looked up. Emily peeked around the door smiling. He could never get enough of simply gazing at her.

"Hi. Can I interrupt?"

"Come on in. I'm getting a head start on my final report." Hearing himself say the word *final* dampened his spirits. He hated to think about how few days he had left here.

"That bad?"

"Better now. I was just thinking about camp closing down."

"I have something else that may cheer you up." With a flourish, she handed him a sheet of the telephone pad paper.

Drew read the name and number she'd written down. He'd been expecting this call. The phone interview he'd had with the bank had gone very well. He waited for the surge of anticipation, the high feeling he used to get when he'd run all of his analyses and was about to see the results that would tell him if his stock pick was a "recommend" for addition to one or more of his former employer's many mutual funds. The rush didn't come.

"The person who called said he'd tried your cell phone first and got dead space."

"Yeah, I gave him the house phone number in case he couldn't reach me here. I'm in and out of the office all day."

"I know your type," she teased. "Why be inside if you can be outdoors. I grew up with a whole family of people like you."

He stood, rested his hands on her waist and gazed down at her. "Admit it. You're coming over to our side. You walked down here instead of driving."

"I admit nothing."

But Emily was much more comfortable here at the lake than she was when he'd first met her. Or did it seem so because that's what he wanted? Of course, that wasn't important if they both were going to be back in the city in a short time. His gaze drifted to the window and the peaks towering in the distance.

"I should get back to work."

"Me, too."

He watched her walk away along the tree-shaded path until he couldn't see her anymore.

Back at his desk, Drew fingered the paper. He picked up the phone, started to dial, then put it down. Maybe he could arrange to work mostly from Paradox. The job the interviewer had talked about was mostly back office work that could be done from anywhere. He could go into New York as needed. Kind of like the arrangement Emily had with the ad agency this summer. If only the possibility of the coalition hiring him to manage the camp full-time wasn't coaxing him to stay. He hadn't mentioned his conversation with Scott to Emily. While she'd stayed a couple of weeks longer to visit with her parents and grandmother, she still seemed bent on getting back to New York City.

His wanting work that would keep him in the mountains, and her wanting to get back to the city, put them both in the same situation his former fiancée had put him. Having to choose between their careers and their relationship. The only way he wasn't going to drive himself crazy over the situation was to give it all up to God.

Lord, I'll abide with Your choice for me.

His simple prayer infused Drew with calm. He picked up the phone and made his call.

When the call ended, Drew tried to drum up some enthusiasm for the job offer and to accept God's direction, as he'd vowed minutes before. The investment bank had offered him an analyst job in New York, starting as soon as he wanted. Emily would be happy. He'd have the means to come up north any time he wanted, assuming he wouldn't be working seventy hours a week. But if the job demanded that much of his time, he wouldn't be able to see her any more than if he had a less demanding job here and she was working in New York.

At least the bank had given him a couple of days to decide whether to take the job. The VP who had made him the offer said that the human resources department would email him the details in writing for him to look over before making his decision. He could still hope that the coalition of churches' pie-in-the-sky plan of running a camp year-round would come through.

Drew closed his report file since he couldn't concentrate on it anyway, and walked up to the house to find Emily attacking the flower beds with a garden claw. "I see you finished your work early, too."

"You might say that." She tore at the roots of a particularly stubborn weed. "Donna emailed me not to worry about making my deadline on the Caramel Crazies account. Amy had some free time and she whipped up a presentation." The claw came down into the soil with a wham.

Drew made a mental note to never to make Emily mad when she had anything sharp or pointed in her hand.

"Why do I put up with it?" she asked.

"The usual reasons. It's your job. It pays for a place to live. You like to eat."

She stood up and wiped her forearm across her forehead. Two spots of dirt adorned her knees. "But I used to enjoy my work. It was fun most of the time." She brushed off the dirt. "I'm sure things will be different once I'm back in New York and in the thick of things."

"If they're not, you could try freelancing."

"I've thought of that. I should do some checking around once we get back to New York."

A small hope glimmered that he could convince her to stay here if he did. With the right contacts, she could freelance almost anywhere, even in Paradox.

She took his hand. "Come on, let's sit on the porch out of this sweltering sun. I'm melting. You can tell me about your job offer. You did get an offer, right?"

"Yes, I did." He wished he could be as enthused about it as she was.

They sat in matching Adirondack chairs. "Tell me all about it." Emily leaned on her elbow on the chair arm closest to him.

"The job is with an investment bank. Financial analysis, like I did before for the mutual funds company."

"When do you start?"

"I can start any time. HR is emailing me the employment contract and more details on the benefits and that stuff."

She jumped up, grabbed his hands and tugged him to his feet. "That's great!" She hugged him.

Much as he hated to leave her embrace, he had to tell her. "I haven't accepted the job."

Her arm-hold loosened.

"As I said, the job is a lot like my last one, which means sixty, seventy hour work weeks and cutthroat pressure to produce. Quite a contrast with working at the camp this summer."

She laid her head on his chest. "We've had a good summer. But you can't vacation up here all the time."

Resentment filled him. His job managing the camp wasn't a vacation. It certainly was as important a job as anything he'd done or could do in the financial sector. Flashes of the kids who'd come to camp over the summer entered his thoughts. What he'd helped give the kids was much more important. Had he read Emily wrong? Was she just like Tara? Would she let his choice of work stonewall their chance at a relationship?

"Maybe I could."

She pulled back and looked up at him.

"Scott called me the other day. The coalition is working to raise enough money to run a camp and conference center in the Adirondacks year-round. If it does, Scott says I'm the first choice for camp manager."

All joy left her face. He resisted the urge to kiss her mindless and erase what he'd told her about the camp job. Nothing was certain. The other job was a firm offer, even if he didn't want to take it.

"But you'd be here and I'd be in New York."

"I'd be back and forth to New York. And you said you were thinking about going out on your own freelancing."

"In New York."

"We could see each other weekends, which is as much or more than you'd get if I take the investment bank position." He stopped himself. He sounded like he was begging. He wouldn't beg.

"Let's not argue about something that hasn't even happened," she said.

And you hope never does. His heart sank.

She slipped away and sat in the chair as stiffly upright as a person could in an Adirondack chair. She looked around as if searching for what to say next. "It sure feels funny without Autumn around."

Evidently Emily was done discussing their situation. He'd let it drop for the moment, but it wasn't over. He had to know whether Emily only cared for him if he was a well-off financial professional. He couldn't reconcile that side of Emily with the woman he'd spent the summer with at Paradox Lake. But, then, he hadn't seen the real side of Tara, either. Could be he was just blind when it came to judging beautiful women.

"Why don't we take a swim in the lake to cool down, and I'll take you out for dinner?"

"Sorry. I can't."

He searched her face to see if she was saying no to get back at him for not locking in the analyst job. No, that was Tara's way, not Emily's.

"Mrs. Donnelly called and asked me if I could cover for her at the Bargain Basement this evening. Her grandson was released from the hospital early and he's arriving home today. She wanted to go to the airport with the rest of the family."

"I thought you didn't do volunteer work at church." His intended tease came out flat, almost harsh.

"The Hazards always volunteer at church. I couldn't refuse." Her retort dripped with sarcasm.

Maybe they should finish the talk about his work and get it out of their systems.

"I mean that. The how could I refuse part." Emily's voice sounded tired. "I'm sure I wasn't the first person she called. What if it was Neal coming home? I'd want to be at the airport. Besides, living here in Paradox as an adult this summer, I can see how people get enjoyment and satisfaction out of volunteering."

Drew went still. That was a big admission for Emily. A crack of hope opened up in his heart that she might be more outwardly averse to life in Paradox than she felt inside.

"Up here in nowhere-land, I mean. Where there's not much else to do."

"You know, it's okay to enjoy the fellowship of working with others. It's even okay to admit to liking parts of small town living. I'm going to go take that swim now."

Drew pushed out of his chair and took the porch steps two at a time. Emily watched him cross the yard to the road with a heavy heart. He couldn't be serious about staying at the lake. Not if he was serious about their relationship. He had to know she couldn't stay here. She didn't fit in. She never had. Granted she had felt comfortable here this summer. But that was because she knew the situation was temporary and didn't care what the locals thought about her.

Except, a small voice in the back of her head said, *people welcomed you, treated you fine.*

She shook off the voice. She had her work. If she didn't get back down to the office, Donna could give her position to someone else, to Amy. Emily couldn't stand for that. She'd worked too hard to get where she was.

But does it make you happy?

She stood abruptly and let her gaze rest on the majestic beauty of the high peaks against the cloudless blue of the late summer sky. Paradox Lake was enchanting as a vacation spot. But her real life was in New York. The life she'd dreamed of for years and left Paradox to successfully pursue.

Drew had to be caught up in the summer mystique, reminiscing about his childhood camp days. Once he got into the routine of his financial work, he'd be fine. They'd be fine. She gave the scenery one last look before going into the house and closing the screen door, ignoring the nagging feeling that she was being dishonest with herself.

Chapter Eighteen

"Good morning," her dad greeted her when she walked into the kitchen the next day.

"Morning." Emily poured herself a cup of coffee and joined her father at the kitchen table.

"I wanted to catch you before you see Drew."

Before I see Drew? What was her father talking about?

"What's up?" she asked.

"It's about the campground. I know you say you don't want to have anything to do with it."

Emily tried to swallow the lump that had formed in her throat. She had been vocal, very vocal, about that since she'd been younger than Autumn. She'd never given much thought about how big a part Lakeside played in her dad's life. It was his career, like her work in New York was hers.

"Your mom and I negotiated a long-term lease with the coalition of churches that's renting it this summer, contingent on their getting the financing they need."

"They want to run their camp year-round," she filled in.

"So Drew did talk with you."

"He mentioned the possibility of a year-round camp." The lump re-formed in her throat. *And of him staying to manage it.*

"Drew's brother, Scott, called me just before you came

down. An anonymous donor came through with all the money the coalition needed."

"Oh, Dad. Are you sure about this, giving up Lakeside?"

"Your mother and I had been thinking about what we'd do when we retired."

"But you're not old enough to retire." Then, it struck her. Money. Mom and Dad had been down in Florida for months taking care of Grandma. "Is it a financial thing? Maybe Neal and I could help."

He laughed. "No, not at all. It's nice of you to offer. We'll get a good income from the rental. And I'm not giving up Lakeside. The coalition has offered me a job overseeing all the maintenance. That should keep me busy enough."

Her father's joy at being back at Paradox Lake shone brightly on his face. She wished she could spend more time here with him and Mom. But Donna was pushing her to return to the office. Emily had thought she and Drew would be going back to New York next week. She swallowed her apprehension.

"Want some breakfast?" her father asked. "I can stir up some more scrambled eggs."

"No. Thanks. I'm going to walk down to the lodge."

"Ah, so that's how it is. It's going to be good having Drew around permanently."

"Right." For him. She would be down in the city. Hadn't he listened to what she'd said yesterday? But her dad couldn't know for sure that Drew had taken the camp job. Dad had said Scott called to say the coalition had gotten its funding. Drew did have that other job offer.

Her footsteps slowed as the lodge came into sight. Drew's truck was parked in front. She breathed in the clean mountain air and marched up the steps. Through the screen door, she saw him in the office working at the computer. Her gaze traced his profile, and her heartbeat tripled in a combination of fear and longing. He looked out the open office door when she creaked the screen door open and smiled. Her nerve and resolve battled to see which could melt faster.

Lord, please, she pleaded silently, not knowing exactly what she was pleading for. In answer, her feet took on a life of their own and moved her, step by step, to the office doorway.

"Hi. I hear congratulations are in order."

"Your dad told you." His tone was perfectly modulated.

She nodded. "Can I sit down or should I come back later when you're less busy?" She gestured at the computer, willing him to tell her to stay. She didn't know if she could make the trip back down here a second time.

"I'm not busy."

She sat in the chair next to his desk.

He stared at her for a moment. "You know I'm going to take the offer from the coalition." A kaleidoscope of emotions flashed across his face.

"I know."

"You're okay with that?" The emotions solidified into a single look of hope that stabbed her like an ice pick.

"No. I thought I'd made myself clear yesterday."

He reached across the table and took her hand. The ripple of electricity that raced through her did nothing to relieve her pain.

"Will you consider staying?"

All of the oxygen left her lungs. She shook her head. "I can't." He really hadn't heard her at all. That didn't bode well for any continuing relationship. Her throat clogged.

"Can't or won't?" His voice took on an edge and he grasped her hand more firmly as if to stop her from leaving.

"Do you even have to ask?" Did he really think she would give up everything she'd worked so hard for so he could play camp a little longer? She bit her lip. That wasn't kind, but she wasn't feeling kind.

"I had to ask. I thought maybe you'd gotten beyond your childish crusade against living here."

Childish? He really didn't know her at all. She pulled her hand from his.

"You've proven that you can do your job here, almost anywhere. It's not like I can manage a large fresh-air camp in New York City."

"To the contrary, this summer has shown me that I can't do my job here. The work Donna has given me the past few months is a parody of what I usually handle." Not that she'd missed the breakneck pace of working in the agency office all that much. But she had missed the creativity of the more complicated campaigns she usually worked on, jobs that Donna had kept in-office.

Drew raised his hand. "Let's not fight. I have to meet with the coalition in a couple of weeks. I'll help you drive your things down. Your subletters will be out by then, right?"

"They're out now. They found a place they could move in right away, rather than having to wait until the first. If I can get a rental vehicle, I thought I'd leave tomorrow."

"I'm sorry, but I can't drop everything and help you pack up." He motioned to the folders on the desk. "I have to finish up the summer camp reports and work up the fall program."

"I'm sure Dad and Autumn and her friends will help." She wasn't sure at all, but now that she'd said she was leaving tomorrow, she wasn't about to change that plan because he was busy.

"Your mind's made up."

She nodded, fearing that if she opened her mouth, she'd stay the extra couple weeks—or months.

His eyes sparked.

Anger or pain?

He pushed his chair back from the desk. "At least we have tonight. I'll see if I can get reservations for that fancy restaurant on Lake George."

"I can't."

"Why? Are you filling in for someone at church again?"

His sarcasm almost undid her. She was losing control of who she was, and if she didn't know who she was, how could she know what she wanted?

She bit the side of her mouth, the sharp pain bolstering her resolve. "No, I don't have other plans. I need time alone to think. It's better if we don't see each other tonight."

"Better for whom?" A muscle worked in his jaw.

"Just better."

"Come on. Be reasonable."

"I am being reasonable. My work is in New York. You had that other offer."

"The camp is a better offer. For me."

"But not for me." She wondered if he had even considered the other job offer. "This conversation isn't going anywhere. I'm going back to the house. We can get together next time you come to New York to meet with the coalition—if you want to."

She turned and left his office. Each step she took tore a piece out of his heart. He knew what he wanted, and was sure that Emily wanted the same thing. She just didn't fully realize it yet. They'd work things out. Unless he was a bigger fool than he'd care to admit. He'd been stupid before with Tara. Was Emily's little drama a ploy to get him to change his mind and take the position at the investment bank? Emily's usually easy-to-read face had been an undecipherable mask. For a nanosecond, he entertained the idea of taking the research analyst job at the investment bank.

But he truly believed it was God's will that he take the camp job. And he wanted to believe that God wouldn't have put Emily in his life if they weren't supposed to be together. Unless Emily really cared for him and not for some picture in her mind of who she thought he was, wanted him to be.

Emily was right. They needed some time apart to think and for her to come to her senses. How could she not see that she belonged in Paradox, not New York, for so many reasons? He'd given his job situation up to the Lord. He needed to muster the steel to do the same with Emily and his relationship. He tried to immerse himself in his report. She'd come to her senses by tomorrow.

He hoped.

Chapter Nineteen

"I still don't see why Drew couldn't tear himself away from his work to help you pack," Autumn complained. "If I were him, I'd be driving you. It's not your fault that you have to go back earlier than you planned."

Emily winced. She hadn't exactly told Autumn that her boss wanted her back today, but she hadn't disabused that assumption, either.

"What kind of boyfriend is he, anyway?" Autumn blessed Jack with a dazzling smile.

None at all was Emily's first thought. He wasn't even trying to understand that she couldn't stay here in Paradox. It was too peaceful, familiar, comforting. Stifling. Paradox was too stifling, she insisted to herself.

"We said goodbye. For now," she added hastily. "He'll be coming to New York soon to meet with the coalition."

"And I'm sure we'll see you up here a lot more now," Emily's dad said as he and Jack lifted her workstation top into the rental SUV.

Even though she wasn't nearly as sure of that as Dad sounded, Emily couldn't help laughing at the way her niece waggled her eyebrows at her.

"That's it," Jack said.

Emily closed the back door. "Thanks. I appreciate you guys helping."

"No problem," Jack said.

"Your mom and I just wish you weren't going back so soon."

"He's right about that," her mother said from behind her. "I've really enjoyed having you here the past couple of weeks."

Emily turned and hugged her. "I've enjoyed being here." She had, and not only the couple of weeks since her parents had returned. She'd enjoyed the whole summer.

She stepped from her mother's embrace. "I'm going to go in and say goodbye to Grandma."

"She's waiting for you in the living room," Mom said.

As Emily walked though the dining room to the living room, a deluge of nostalgia swept through her. Growing up on Paradox Lake hadn't been all bad. She'd always known her family loved her, even if she walked a different path than they, and seemingly everyone one else in Paradox, did. And she'd never carried the small nugget of fear for her safety that she carried with her in the city. A nugget that made living there all the more exciting. Didn't it?

Her grandmother was seated in the recliner, a novel open on her lap.

"I've got to get going, Grandma."

She closed her book. "I could have come out to say goodbye, but I wanted a minute alone with you."

Emily steeled herself for Grandma to press her to stay.

"I like your friend Drew."

Not what Emily had expected. "I do, too." That was true, even though she was mad at him and hurt that he wasn't trying to see her side.

"I'm sure you think going back to New York is the right thing to do."

"It's my job."

Her grandmother raised her hand. "Let me finish. Are you going back because you want to or think you have to? Are you still trying to prove that you're not little Jinx Hazard anymore? Everyone knows that but you."

Emily clenched and unclenched her fists. Grandma didn't understand, either. Or was she right? Emily didn't know anymore.

"Now, give me a hug and a kiss and get going. But promise me one—no, two—things. You'll pray on your decision and listen to the answer you get. And you'll come see me here a lot more than you did when I was in Florida."

"Yes, Grandma." Emily hugged her tight, breathing in the vanilla scent of her lotion that always reminded Emily of baking sugar cookies. "See you soon."

"I hope so. Drive safe."

On her way out, Emily touched one of her mother's kitschy dishtowels. Some things never changed. But she and Paradox Lake had. Emily hadn't felt like an outsider this summer, despite her years away at college and New York. She'd been more at home than when she'd lived here. A last glance around brought tears to the corners of her eye. She blinked them away. But it wasn't home. Home was her job at the ad agency and her apartment in New York City. Maybe someday, she allowed. When she was better established. She could have a second home here. Emily stepped out and breathed the fresh scent of pine. A girl could dream.

Her gaze moved to the pickup truck where everyone stood waiting to say goodbye to her. Almost everyone. She turned away, past the truck toward the lake. An empty part inside her looked for Drew heading up the road to see her off, even though she'd asked him not to. The trees beside the empty road rustled.

She looked up at the clear blue sky. *Lord, I made the only choice I could. Didn't I?*

* * *

The drive down to the city was uneventful and Emily was able to find a parking spot not too far from the agency's building.

She'd planned to take a day to settle in, start work tomorrow. But when she'd talked with Donna yesterday, the art director had insisted that Emily come in today. She'd made a big deal about some announcement that she and the partners were making today. Emily *had* to be there for the two o'clock meeting. She'd been too off balance from her talk with Drew to think about why Donna hadn't mentioned this big announcement before.

She hardly recognized the agency when she walked into the reception area. The bright orange and red accents had been replaced by serene blues and greens.

A new receptionist looked up and asked, "Can I help you?"

"I'm Emily Hazard."

The receptionist looked at her blankly.

"I'm the assistant art director. I've been out on family leave."

"Oh, I thought Amy…"

"Emily!" Donna stepped from her office into the reception area. "You're back."

Strains of the theme song from the old *Twilight Zone* reruns she'd watched on TV as a kid played in her head. Donna had told her to come in today. "Yes, I'm back. Do you want to get together after I settle in my office?"

"About your office…" Donna started.

"Oh, is it being redecorated?" Emily motioned to the changes in the reception area.

"No, that's already finished. I think you'll like it."

As if she had a choice. Emily was sure Donna had initiated the redecorating, and whatever Donna decided was pretty much law in the art department.

Emily took a step toward her office.

"It's just that Amy has been using your office while you were gone."

Emily stopped short. "What?"

Donna pushed her hair back behind her ear. "She was working on a lot of your projects."

Not by my choice.

"It was easier for everyone." Her boss couldn't have given her a more insincere smile if an Academy Award depended on it.

"So, what? I have to work in one of the freelancer cubicles until Amy gets her stuff out of my office?" Why did Donna insist she come in today if they weren't ready for her to be back?

"Of course not. Everyone's in the conference room waiting for you."

That's right. The big announcement.

Her apprehension lifted as they walked down the hall. Maybe her coworkers were giving her a surprise welcome back party. They stepped through the doorway. No one jumped and yelled "surprise." Rather, they were all seated around the table looking like she'd felt a minute ago. Except Amy. Emily's breakfast bagel and second cup of coffee weighed heavily in her stomach.

Donna took the chair at the head of the polished mahogany table next to Amy and indicated Emily should sit on her other side. The executive partners sat at the opposite end of the table.

"First," Donna said, "let's welcome Emily back."

Everyone clapped politely. Emily stretched her lips into a forced smile. They could have been a little more enthusiastic. But it wasn't like they were all close friends. They were coworkers.

"All right. Now for our announcement," Donna said.

The guys at the opposite end of the table nodded.

"We're pleased to announce that Amy Watson has been promoted to assistant art director."

Emily went cold, and it had nothing to do with the air conditioning. She was the assistant art director.

As if programmed, the room broke into loud applause. Emily mechanically brought her palms together as if clapping two forty pound weights.

"And," Donna continued, "with my promotion to partner…"

Donna was a partner? When had that happened?

"The art director position is open."

Did she dare hope? Emily couldn't take her eyes off Donna for fear she'd read something different in the other partners' faces.

"We're hoping Emily will agree to fill it. Emily?"

Art director? When she'd graduated from college that had been part of her five-year plan. To make art director at a smaller agency, as a stepping stone to bigger things. Hadn't she told herself she wanted to be Donna? So where was the excitement, the satisfaction? It must be the surprise of it all.

"I…I'm… Sure, yes, I accept."

"Excellent," Donna said. The other partners congratulated Emily.

Once again, the room broke into applause. But to Emily, it sounded more muted than the applause for Amy.

"We're done, then," Donna said. She turned to Emily as the others started filing out. "I'm thrilled you agreed."

"I'm thrilled you asked." She *was* thrilled, wasn't she?

"You'll be in my old office. I had your desk and things moved in."

Donna must have been pretty confident she'd take the job.

"For today, I've left you folders on all our current jobs in progress, so you can bring yourself up to speed. Tomorrow, I can go over your duties more thoroughly. I'm tied up with meetings all day today."

Donna wanted her to start working today? "Uh, I thought I'd go over to my apartment now and unload my stuff. Start work tomorrow morning."

"Don't worry about your stuff. My nephews will meet you at your apartment at five-thirty to carry your things up to your place." Donna smiled as if she'd given Emily a wonderful gift.

"I was going to have my super help me."

"And now you don't have to. You've been gone half the year already."

"Four months."

"Whatever. I need you up to speed pronto. Talk to you later." Donna headed down the opposite hall and Emily made her way to her new office. Except for Emily's desk and file cabinet and a fresh coat of beige paint, the room looked exactly as it had when Donna occupied it. The agency redecorating must not have come this far down the hall. She sat and opened the first folder.

At five, she was about halfway through the files.

Donna poked her head in the door. "Hey, why don't you call it a day? My nephews will be over at your place soon. And you probably want to go out and celebrate."

"You sure?" Emily often worked well past five, and Donna was usually still there.

"The work will still be here tomorrow." Donna grinned. "I'd go celebrate with you, but I have a dinner meeting tonight."

Celebrate. Right. With who? Everyone she cared about, who cared about her, was in Paradox Lake. Emily closed the file she'd been reading and stared at it. Grandma's words came back to her. *Give it up to God.* Suddenly, she knew what she had to do.

Emily drove past her apartment building and finally found a parking place nearly a block away. She walked back. As she approached her building, she saw a man leaning against the wrought iron stair railing. Her heart raced.

"Drew! What are you doing here?"

"Waiting for you. Your grandmother called as soon as you'd left this morning. I didn't think you'd really leave like that."

"And you've been waiting here all afternoon?"

"Yeah, in my truck." He grinned and pointed across the street.

"You know," he said. "I did listen to what you said yesterday. I just didn't think you meant it. Obviously, you did. So here I am."

Drew's admission warmed her heart. It couldn't have been easy for him.

Emily started. "You didn't quit your job at the camp, did you?"

He blanched. "I tried, but Scott wouldn't accept my resignation." He rushed on. "The distance isn't that great. We can have weekends together, and I'll have to come to New York. A lot."

He really was adorable. "No."

Drew winced.

She had to quit torturing him. "Because I quit my job at the ad agency."

"For real?"

"For real."

He opened his arms, and she stepped into his embrace. He held her close and kissed the top of her head. "That wasn't nice."

"I know, but I couldn't resist."

He removed one arm from around her waist and reached in his pocket.

What was he doing?

He released his other arm, and she let go a little squeak of protest at the loss of their shared warmth.

Drew went down on one knee in front of her, one hand hidden behind his back.

He wasn't.

He brought his hand in front and flipped open the small black velvet box he held.

He was.

"I love you, Emily Jinx Hazard. Will you do me the honor of being my wife?"

The love shining in his light blue eyes stopped the grin prompted by his formal words before it spread to her lips.

"Yes," she whispered. "I love you, too. And I'd be honored to be your wife."

He slipped the ring on her finger and pulled her into his arms for a long, thorough kiss.

A catcall from across the street pulled them apart.

"I'd better get going," Emily said.

"You have plans for tonight?"

Emily was hard-pressed not to laugh at his bemused expression.

"I sure do. The car rental place is open until seven. Once I return the SUV, we're heading home to Paradox Lake."

Five hours later Drew turned off State Route 74 onto the campground road. He gently shook Emily's shoulder and woke her from her light sleep.

"We're home," he said.

Emily blinked and saw Paradox Lake ahead. The moonlight sparkled on the calm blue water. She turned to Drew. Just having him beside her filled her with a quiet peace.

"Yes, we're finally home."

* * * * *

Dear Reader,

I'm thrilled to be part of the Love Inspired family with the publication of *Small-Town Sweethearts*.

One question authors are frequently asked is where we get our story ideas. The idea for *Small-Town Sweethearts* came from a conversation with a family member who told me how much she liked their new church because the service and the people were more formal, and she could worship privately there. In contrast, I really like our church because of the fellowship the congregation shares.

I started thinking about the value of Christian fellowship and how different people may perceive it, and the story unfolded. My choice of Paradox Lake in the Adirondack Mountains of Northern New York for the setting comes from a lifelong love of my "hometown" Upstate New York and a personal quest to introduce the world-at-large to the wide expanse of New York State outside of the New York City area. I hope to visit Paradox Lake again soon in my writing.

Thanks so much for choosing *Small-Town Sweethearts*. Please feel free to email me at JeanCGordon@yahoo.com or snail mail me c/o Harlequin Love Inspired, 233 Broadway, Suite 1001, New York, NY 10279. You can also visit me at Facebook.com/JeanCGordon.Author or www.JeanCGordon.com.

Jean C. Gordon

Questions for Discussion

1. Emily believes she doesn't fit in with the people in Paradox Lake because of the way she remembers childhood incidents. Do you think she has exaggerated her feelings of being a high school misfit? Or did her classmates actually bully her with their teasing?

2. Should Emily's parents have discouraged the use of the nickname Jinx?

3. Emily has concerns about her niece, Autumn, not wanting to broaden her horizons. How does this affect their relationship?

4. Have you ever thought you knew what was best for a family member and later realized he or she needed to live his or her own life? How did you feel?

5. Drew thinks that his mother sees him as the family's financial support and his older brother, Scott, as the spiritual support. How does this affect the choices Drew makes and how he feels about those choices?

6. Emily says she prefers a more formal worship service than Hazardtown Community Church offers. Do you think this is true or that Emily isn't being totally honest with herself? Why?

7. Have you ever had a preconceived idea of how a worship service should be or about some other aspect of your faith that has prevented you from being open to a different way of worshipping or to understanding someone else's beliefs?

8. When Emily's niece, Autumn, is upset about her father possibly being missing or injured in Afghanistan, Drew wants her to join with him and Emily in a prayer for Neal and the others. When Autumn is resistant, Emily tells Drew to leave her alone and let her pray privately if she wants to. Drew thinks Autumn needs their prayer support. Who do you think is right?

9. Emily begins the book thinking that you can't go home again or at least that she doesn't want to. Have you gone back to some place you visited or lived in when you were a child or teenager and found it wasn't as you'd remembered it? How did you feel?

10. The longer Emily stays in Paradox Lake, the more comfortable she is there. Do you think Emily changes, or has Paradox Lake changed?

11. What part do you think Emily and Drew's relationship has on her feeling more comfortable in Paradox Lake?

12. How does Emily's parents' return to Paradox Lake affect the decisions she makes?

13. Drew gives his job situation decision up to God. Why do you think Emily has a harder time doing the same?

14. Drew seems to have an easier time making a decision about his career and about his feelings for Emily than Emily does. Why?

15. Some people might see Emily's return to Paradox Lake with Drew as giving up on her career goals. Do you agree? Why or why not?

16. The author chose Matthew 18:20 as representative of the story. Do you agree? Why or why not? Do you have another verse you think is more relevant?

INSPIRATIONAL

Wholesome romances that touch the heart and soul.

Love Inspired®

celebrating
15
YEARS

COMING NEXT MONTH
AVAILABLE JANUARY 31, 2012

HOMETOWN HEARTS
The Granger Family Ranch
Jillian Hart

THE LAST BRIDGE HOME
Redemption River
Linda Goodnight

SECOND CHANCE MATCH
Chatam House
Arlene James

ROCKY POINT PROMISE
Barbara McMahon

FALLING FOR THE FIREMAN
Allie Pleiter

A HOUSE FULL OF HOPE
Missy Tippens

Look for these and other Love Inspired books wherever books
are sold, including most bookstores, supermarkets, discount
stores and drug stores.   LICNM0112

REQUEST YOUR FREE BOOKS!

2 FREE INSPIRATIONAL NOVELS
PLUS 2
FREE
MYSTERY GIFTS

Love Inspired.

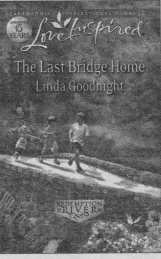

Louisa Morgan loves being around children.
So when she has the opportunity to tutor bedridden Ellie,
she's determined to bring joy back into the motherless
girl's world. Can she also help Ellie's father open his
heart again? Read on for a sneak peek of

THE COWBOY FATHER

by Linda Ford,
available February 2012 from Love Inspired Historical.

Why had Louisa thought she could do this job? A bubble of self-pity whispered she was totally useless, but Louisa ignored it. She wasn't useless. She could help Ellie if the child allowed it.

Emmet walked her out, waiting until they were out of earshot to speak. "I sense you and Ellie are not getting along."

"Ellie has lost her freedom. On top of that, everything is new. Familiar things are gone. Her only defense is to exert what little independence she has left. I believe she will soon tire of it and find there are more enjoyable ways to pass the time."

He looked doubtful. Louisa feared he would tell her not to return. But after several seconds' consideration, he sighed heavily. "You're right about one thing. She's lost everything. She can hardly be blamed for feeling out of sorts."

"She hasn't lost everything, though." Her words were quiet, coming from a place full of certainty that Emmet was more than enough for this child. "She has you."

"She'll always have me. As long as I live." He clenched his fists. "And I fully intend to raise her in such a way that even if something happened to me, she would never feel like I was gone. I'd be in her thoughts and in her actions every day."

Peace filled Louisa. "Exactly what my father did."

Their gazes connected, forged a single thought about fathers and daughters…how each needed the other. How sweet the relationship was.

Louisa tipped her head away first. "I'll see you tomorrow."

Emmet nodded. "Until tomorrow then."

She climbed behind the wheel of their automobile and turned toward home. She admired Emmet's devotion to his child. It reminded her of the love her own father had lavished on Louisa and her sisters. Louisa smiled as fond memories of her father filled her thoughts. Ellie was a fortunate child to know such love.

Louisa understands what both father and daughter are going through. Will her compassion help them heal—and form a new family? Find out in
THE COWBOY FATHER
by Linda Ford, available February 14, 2012.